THE SANCTUARY

City lawyer Kimberley is forced to take over an animal sanctuary left to her in a will. The Sanctuary, a Victorian house overlooking the sea, draws Kimberley under its spell. The same cannot be said for her husband Scott, whose dedication to his work threatens their relationship. When Kimberley comes to the aid of handsome, brooding widower Zach Coen and his troubled daughter, she could possibly help them. But will she risk endangering her marriage in the process?

CARA COOPER

THE SANCTUARY

Complete and Unabridged

LINFORD
Leicester

First published in Great Britain in 2009

First Linford Edition
published 2010

British Library CIP Data

Cooper, Cara.
　The sanctuary.- -(Linford romance library)
　1. Women lawyers- -Fiction.
　2. Animal sanctuaries- -Fiction.
　3. Widowers- -Fiction. 4. Love stories
　5. Large type books.
　I. Title II. Series
　823.9'2–dc22

ISBN 978–1–84782–982–5

Published by
F. A. Thorpe (Publishing)
Anstey, Leicestershire

Set by Words & Graphics Ltd.
Anstey, Leicestershire
Printed and bound in Great Britain by
T. J. International Ltd., Padstow, Cornwall

This book is printed on acid-free paper

Kimberley Receives A Letter

'Come on, Kimberley, you don't have time to look at the post now, you promised to drive me to my meeting and I'm late already!'

Kimberley Wright stared at the envelope that was franked with the name of a solicitors' firm in Hampshire. Why on earth would she be getting a letter from that neck of the woods? She didn't know anybody in Hampshire, although she vaguely remembered her mother talking about a holiday somewhere near the sea when Kimberley was a toddler.

She longed to open the envelope, but Scott was standing impatiently in front of her by the door, briefcase at his side and an expression which told her that any minute he was about to boil over.

'Sorry,' she said, and threw the pile of post onto the hall table.

'It's all right for you,' Scott's voice had that testy note to it that she knew spelled out stress with a capital 'S.' He opened the front door to their flat and set off down the elegant mirrored hallway, hastily adjusting his tie and running his fingers through his dark hair. He looked every inch the smart young lawyer that he was.

Kimberley locked their flat door behind her and ran to catch him up. 'What do you mean, it's all right for me?'

'Now you're working from home, you appear to have lost all sense of time.'

His words stung her. She'd been ready before him. She'd even brought him tea in bed this morning, aware that he had a big day ahead. He'd been the one who had lain there, talking about his meeting today.

Scott was desperate for a partnership in the law firm he had been with since leaving university, and this new case he was to work on, might, if all went well, clinch a promotion for him.

2

'I have not lost all sense of time, Scott.' Kimberley breathed deeply, trying to keep calm. 'Actually, now I work from home, I find I need to be *more* disciplined with my time, not less.'

'Hmph,' was the only answer her husband gave her.

She watched him jabbing at the lift buttons as if pressing harder would make it come more quickly. Little patches of sweat started to bead on his brow, and she saw the emergence of the daily frown that seemed to carve itself into his face every time he set off for work. Kimberley wished Scott wouldn't pace up and down in front of the lift like that. His knuckles were white as he held his briefcase, and she wondered whether all this anxiety was really worth it. Her eyes settled on the plush velvet brown carpet which lay over cream coloured marble tiles. A huge bowl of white lilies stood on a table in an alcove, tasteful, luxurious. This building was immaculate. Their flat, in the centre of London's Barbican, was amongst some of the most expensive real estate in the country. For Scott, living here proved they had made it. But it all needed paying for. And at what price? Kimberley couldn't help thinking.

Finally the lift arrived, they stepped in and it whispered down to the underground car park. Kimberley made her voice light; 'I'll do us something special for dinner tonight.'

'We can go out.'

Kimberley could see that Scott wasn't really concentrating; his mind was already on his big meeting. And, what's more, by his off-hand tone, she suspected that he had forgotten that today was their third anniversary. Unless, of course, she tried to persuade herself, maybe he was just pretending to forget. That was it, of course. He was only pretending. He would come home tonight with a bunch of roses and a bottle of champagne. 'No, let's not go out,' she said, as she drove out of the underground car park, 'I'll cook for us, do us something nice.'

'If you want,' said Scott. 'Although I don't know why you bother to cook. It seems to take ages and create mountains of washing-up. And by the time you've spent money on all those fancy ingredients, you might just as well pay a restaurant to come up with something better.'

'Something better.'

'Well, not necessarily better,' he put his hand on her arm, realising he might have been less than tactful, 'but something easier.'

'I like cooking for you. It may not be as fancy as eating out but I think it can be just as special. More special, in some ways.'

But Scott had opened his briefcase and taken out a huge wodge of spiral-bound papers littered with brightly-coloured Post-its where he had read and studied and re-read the documents in preparation for his meeting. 'Fine, if it makes you happy, then cook.'

Kimberley's fingers tightened over the steering wheel. Could it be possible that it was only their third anniversary and he hadn't remembered? No, no it couldn't, she told herself, as she weaved through the traffic. He couldn't have changed that much.

On their first anniversary he had given her a card with a beautiful scene of the sun setting over St Mark's Square. Inside it had said, 'Darling Kimberley, every day I thank Heaven that I married the most beautiful girl in the world. So, for the most beautiful girl, let me take you to the most beautiful place in the world. Venice.' That very afternoon he had whisked her off in a taxi to the airport.

They had drunk champagne on the plane, and after they had touched down in Italy, a water taxi had taken them on the magical journey into Venice. With Scott's arms round her like a warm cloak, feeling the gentle bobbing of the water taxi as they both looked out on the gentle waves of the lagoon, she had felt she could never be happier.

Now, Kimberley looked over at her husband as they crawled through the London traffic. If anything, he was even better looking now. His jaw was squarer and more determined. His shoulders were broader, more muscular than when they'd married. He worked out regularly at the gym at his office and sometimes swam in the small pool attached to their block of flats. 'Work hard, play hard,' that had become the motto Scott had adopted. But sometimes she wondered whether the work was taking up more space in his life than the play.

She sighed, and then checked herself. She must support him as he had supported her in the past.

★   ★   ★

'Do you feel you're ready for today?' she asked. 'You've always been a terrific lawyer, Scott, the meeting's bound to go well.'

'Unfortunately, things don't just go well by themselves, you have to work at it,' he said tersely.

'But you spent all yesterday evening and half the night looking at those papers. Maybe you should give yourself a break.'

He leant over and put his hand on Kimberley's shoulder as they approached the office. 'The only break I need is the big break that winning this contract is going to give me. And us Kimberley, and us. Think about it. If this goes well and they give me the partnership, we could afford a house in the country as well as the flat. You've always said you wanted to live in the country. We could find a lovely place, not too far from London, and spend weekends and holidays there and maybe then . . . 'He hesitated, as if he had stepped over an invisible line, his blue grey eyes full of concern for her. She knew what he was going to say, and she straightened her back, ready for it: 'maybe then we might have a baby. Maybe relaxing in the countryside would make it happen.'

* ★ ★

Kimberley bit her lip as she manoeuvred the BMW into a space near Scott's building. It was a sore subject. They'd been trying for a baby ever since they'd married. Three long years and nothing had happened. Tests had come up negative; there was nothing amiss with either of them. It simply wasn't happening. At thirty-three, she was aware of her biological clock not just ticking, but beginning to chime as loudly as Big Ben. That was one of the reasons she'd decided to work at home. Kimberley was a lawyer every bit as successful as Scott, but she was convinced that her hectic lifestyle had contributed to her not being able to have a child.

She had been drained by constantly running around from one meeting to another, being forever on a knife-edge. Jamming a phone handset under her chin, taking one call while hastily making amendments to contracts on her computer, had led to her being strung out twenty-four hours a day.

Kimberley had to admit it to herself. She was too dedicated to her work and always sought to give one hundred and ten per cent.

She and Scott certainly had that in common.

When her company had agreed she could work at home, she'd breathed a huge sigh of relief. The pace was slower and less demanding and she no longer had to battle with the frustrating journey to work and the office politics. Kimberley produced the same amount of work and her employers were delighted. She was happy.

But the longed-for pregnancy still hadn't materialised.

'A home in the country is a nice idea,' she said now, as Scott pushed his papers back into his briefcase and snapped it shut, 'but not if it means you having to work too hard.'

'I was made for hard work,' he grinned, as he leant over, planted a kiss on her cheek and eased his long legs out of the car. 'Thanks for the lift. See you later.'

And before she could say goodbye, he'd disappeared through the revolving doors into the glass and steel office.

* * *

Kimberley carefully steered the BMW back out into the traffic and set off for the supermarket. She made a mental list of the things she needed. She was going to make the same meal she'd made for their second anniversary, and as she pushed her trolley round, it made her smile to think of last year's celebration.

That time, she'd surprised Scott by buying a ride in a hot-air balloon. He'd loved every minute of it, letting the breeze take them where it would. The noise of the burners firing up to make then go higher had made them both jump and collapse in each others' arms, laughing like children. They'd landed in a field of lush grass, their hearts pounding at the excitement of the touchdown. Hand in hand they'd started the half hour walk back to their car.

On the way, passing through deserted beech woodland, Scott had impulsively asked Kimberley to sit with him on the moss covered ground in a dip surrounded by cow parsley. There, giggling and whispering, they had lain down and gazed at the sky.

Lying back and listening to the buzzing of the insects and the gentle singing of the birds, Scott had whispered, 'you mean everything to me,' and then pressed a diamond eternity ring into her hand.

She'd turned it around, watching the diamonds glisten as the sunbeams sprinkled on them through the trees, then felt the warmth of his hand as he'd taken the ring from her and threaded it on to her finger.

★　★　★

As if she was on automatic pilot, Kimberley placed courgettes and peppers in her trolley, then steaks and French bread, all the while thinking back to that glorious, sun-filled day.

When they'd got back to the car after the balloon ride, she had shown Scott a hamper with all the things she had bought for a barbecue on the nearby beach. Exactly the same ingredients as today, simple, wholesome, nothing as fancy as the expensive restaurants they could afford to eat in now, but somehow a million times more enjoyable.

Kimberley put a bag of salad into her trolley, followed by some strawberries and cream and she was nearly done. At home she already had the butter, sugar and flour she needed to make the shortbread biscuits. She would use exactly the same recipe as she had for their special meal on that second anniversary.

Thinking of how Scott was that day had made her glow inside. Of course he hadn't forgotten their anniversary, he was just stringing her along, she thought, smiling as she made her way to the checkout. Scott wouldn't forget something as important as their wedding anniversary. One of the reasons she had married him was because he was so romantic and caring. He probably had some big surprise lined up for her. But even if he hadn't, she mused, loading her shopping into bags, it wouldn't matter. She didn't need big gestures. Just a card, or even just a hug and him wishing her a 'Happy Anniversary,' would be enough. He was all she needed.

Besides, she understood how important today's meeting was, and knew how much preparation he had done for it. He wouldn't have had time for big gestures, but maybe he'd have time to pick up a bunch of flowers on the way home. That would be fine, just fine.

Some Astonishing News.

When Kimberley got back to the flat, the first thing she saw as she put her keys on the hall table was the pile of letters she'd tossed there.

She'd forgotten all about the letter from the solicitor's in Hampshire. Now, she gazed at the envelope as she hung up her coat and put her bags in the kitchen. The shopping could wait a few minutes before she put it away.

'Mr Mitchellson, Steyning & Co., Solicitors, Alton, Hampshire.' Being a solicitor herself, Kimberley had had dealings with dozens of solicitor's firms, but none in Alton. She put aside the rest of the post, noticing a pink envelope with her mother's handwriting, which would undoubtedly be an anniversary card. She strolled through the grey-carpeted hallway into the lounge. This was her favourite room in the flat, white walls, white leather sofa and a spiral staircase leading up to the roof garden.

Kimberley sat down and tore open the envelope. Mitchellson, Steyning & Co's letterhead was old-fashioned, in a Gothic script beloved of small town solicitors. So unlike the sparse, clean-lined lettering of the London solicitors she usually dealt with.

As Kimberley read the contents of the letter, she felt her eyes growing wider. She folded the letter, put it down on the sofa, then unfolded and read it again, this time more carefully. She blinked, as if by doing so, the words on the page might make better sense. But a second reading only confirmed the information her brain had taken in the first time.

She didn't know how long she had been sitting there, but she was conscious that the grey clouds that had hung over the early morning had cleared and now the sun was high in the sky and pouring through the elegant

French windows, warming her. The sun seemed to wake her from her astonished reverie, prompting her to pick up the phone. Her hands were shaking as she dialled and she nearly dropped the hand piece. Finally, she heard a click and her mother's familiar voice. 'Kimberley, darling, how lovely to hear from you. Happy anniversary.'

'Thanks Mum, but that's not what I called about.'

'Are you calling about the letter?'

'Did you get one too?' Of course, thought Kimberley, she wouldn't be the only one; her mother would have got one as well.

'Yes I did, darling. Poor Cousin Grace, I didn't even know she was ill, let alone that she'd died. She'd kept herself so much to herself. We'd almost completely lost touch, apart from the annual family newsletter I sent her.'

'Cousin Grace,' Kimberley said, shaking her head slowly. The solicitor's letter had talked about a Grace Drake, and Kimberley simply couldn't place her, but now a glimmer of memory started to filter through.

A large house, set on a hill overlooking a cove. Steps up the hill to the front door. A donkey living on the hill, braying a 'hello' to visitors. Cousin Grace, small, wide-eyed, her hair always held in tight crisp curls which never moved.

Kimberley's mother's voice invaded her childhood memories. 'I've just come off the phone to the solicitors. Apparently Grace was physically and mentally well, but then she had a fall. Complications set in and she never pulled through. Poor Grace. I wish I could have helped. I tried to keep in touch for a long time, but she got so that she wouldn't return my letters. She'd almost become a recluse. In the end there was just her, that huge old house and her animals. They'd come to mean everything to her.'

'Mum.' Kimberley was bursting with her own information. 'Did you know that she's left me something in her will, some sanctuary? I kept on reading it but it didn't make sense.'

'She's left you The Sanctuary? My goodness, that's extraordinary. I wonder what condition the old place is in now?'

'What is The Sanctuary?' Kimberley's head was in a whirl.

'Why, Drake's Sanctuary is that great big old house on the Isle of Wight! Don't you remember? We went there a few times when you were small. You wouldn't have been older than two or three, so I suppose it's not surprising you don't remember it. I've got some photos of you somewhere, running along the beach and building sand-castles.'

Kimberley looked out through the French windows over her balcony and away across the city below with its mad racing traffic and teeming streets full of people. The calm of this flat was her sanctuary.

'Grace didn't have the easiest of lives,' her mother was saying. 'And, well . . . some things happened to her which made her want to retreat from the world. Her family weren't the only ones she didn't keep in touch with. She simply didn't want the company of people. She'd always loved animals, though, and always made them part of her life. She got a bit of a reputation for taking in waifs and strays, and eventually she turned the house into an animal sanctuary. There's a lot of land comes with it, so I guess that's where she kept them all. I wonder who's looking after them now?'

'I've no idea,' Kimberley's voice sounded small and far away, even to herself. It was a lot to take in. 'Maybe they've all been found homes. Perhaps Cousin Grace ran the sanctuary down as she got older.' Kimberley looked again at the letter in her hand. 'It says here that there are certain conditions attached to the legacy and the solicitors have invited me down to Hampshire for a proper reading of the will to talk me through them.'

'It was a strange, ramshackle old

place. I always used to think Grace must have rattled around like a pea on a drum, but she loved it. What will you do with it, dear?'

'I don't have any idea what I'll do with it,' Kimberley said. 'Certainly not until I've seen it, and not until I've heard exactly what these mysterious conditions are. And I really can't think why Cousin Grace would leave it to me when she must hardly have remembered me. Why would she have chosen me, Mum?'

'I don't know, dear. But she must have had her reasons. Although she'd retreated from the world, we used to keep in touch once a year by Christmas card and I'd always send her our round robin family letter updating everybody about what we were up to. She'd been a professional woman herself, some kind of accountant, so she probably admired you. I'm afraid I've always gone on about you in my family letter. I used to update everybody on what you were doing at school, then at uni, and I was always proud of what you've achieved at work.'

'She did leave your father and I some jewellery, which we're very grateful for. She was your father's cousin, not mine, and he was rather fond of her. We knew her very well at one time, so I suppose she felt some connection to our side of the family.'

'I'd like to go down and speak to the solicitors as soon as possible,' Kimberley said. 'Would you come with me, Mum? If I fix it for tomorrow, could you do that?'

'Yes, of course. Being retired has its advantages. Let me know what train you want to catch, and I'll meet you at the station.'

'Great. I'll ring you back.'

★ ★ ★

Kimberley sat back feeling shell-shocked but touched by the extraordinary news. Why had some strange, reclusive, animal lady who she hadn't met in years left her, Kimberley Wright, most of her worldly goods? Sure, Kimberley liked animals. In fact, she and Scott discussed her wish for a cat when they moved into the flat. But Scott liked the clean lines and minimalism of their décor, it went with their professional lifestyle, he said. A cat would leave hairs everywhere and claw the carpets.

'Besides,' he'd reminded her, 'would it really be fair if we haven't got a garden?'

'I suppose you're right, but then a cat would be able to go on the balcony and out on the roof garden.'

'True, and catch birds and bring them back to spread feathers and dirt all over our white sofas.'

'Maybe we wouldn't have the kind of cat which catches birds. Not all of them do, you know.' Kimberley had felt quite upset about them not being able to have a pet, even though she knew what Scott was saying made sense.

Kimberley remembered the cat she'd had as a child, a fluff ball with a white bib and white paws. She recalled the sheer fascination of watching him wash, and trying to capture his many contortions on her sketchpad. Cats were such beautiful creatures and such an honour to own. Even if you gave them the freedom to go out of the house, they always chose you by coming back. And they were so lovely to hold and cuddle.

'Anyway,' Scott had pushed his point home, 'once you get pregnant, you might feel differently about having a cat. Would you want all that mess and trouble of changing litter trays if you wanted to keep the flat clean for a baby?'

That alone had changed Kimberley's mind. Although it was a large flat, it would have perhaps felt too small to have a cat to trip over if she was holding a baby. If she had a baby, that would be the most important thing to her. If . . .

Kimberley got up, went to the window to look out at the hectic city and the people walking briskly in the sunshine, and hugged her arms tightly around herself. That awful longing, that searing desire to hold something small and warm and living swept over her like a giant wave and then passed, leaving an empty, cavernous feeling in her soul. *Don't go there*, she told herself, *don't let yourself start brooding on what you don't have. Focus on what you do have: Scott, this beautiful home and now, this out-of-the-blue legacy.*

★ ★ ★

She turned away from the window and made her way into the kitchen, grabbing her bags of shopping as she did so. Putting the vegetables in the rack and the steaks in the fridge, Kimberley's mind turned to Cousin Grace. Trying to fathom out the mystery of why she had made her a bequest, took her thoughts away from the other things on her mind. Even the thought that Scott might have forgotten their anniversary seemed not to loom quite so heavily on the horizon. He loved her and she him, so what would one forgotten date matter? If he had forgotten, that is.

★ ★ ★

Kimberley shut the kitchen doors firmly and mentally chided herself. Brooding wasn't good. Briskly, she made her way to the office at the back of the flat where her computer sat at a clear Perspex desk below shelves of neat white files containing all her papers. The office, with its clear polished surfaces and carefully stored telephone numbers in a giant Rolodex, reflected Kimberley's organised approach. She had work to do and she must remain focussed on that. Burying herself in her work had been one of the tactics Kimberley had used to forget her childless status before, and it would help her now.

As an employment lawyer, contracts were one of her main concerns.

Smoothing her no-nonsense black skirt and unbuttoning the sleeves of her white shirt to roll them up, Kimberley set to. She had a pile of complex contracts to work through, and putting on her glasses, the ones Scott said made her look studious, but still beautiful, she methodically amended and corrected until lunch-time.

A tuna salad and a half hour in front of the television refreshed her. She allowed herself a few more minutes to open the pile of post, which had lain forgotten on the hallway table, crowded out by the events of the morning. Kimberley smiled briefly at the anniversary cards she and Scott had received, some funny, some touching, then gathered them in a pile and took them into her office, leaving them on the windowsill. Later on, when she was less busy, she would put them out in the lounge.

The afternoon was full of phone calls and e-mails to the companies she advised, and Kimberley found herself immersed in the business of her working day. On her orderly list, though, she had not forgotten to write in the necessity of phoning the Alton lawyers about the legacy, and she arranged a meeting with them for her and her mother the next day. They would go down on the early train.

★ ★ ★

As the afternoon ticked on, and the forget-me-not blue sky gave way to a deep azure, Kimberley looked, startled, at her watch. Scott would be home soon, and she wanted to make their anniversary evening really special.

Putting the finishing touches to the contract she was working on, she saved the document and closed down her computer. After hurrying into the kitchen and putting a bottle of champagne in the fridge, she skipped quickly to the bedroom with its en-suite bathroom and ran herself a bath, tipping in some of her favourite Chanel

19 bath essence. While the scent of the tub filling permeated the bedroom, she made her way to the walk-in closet. She knew exactly what she was going to wear tonight.

Today had been a perfect warm spring day, just like their wedding day, just like their two previous anniversaries. For the balloon trip on their last anniversary, Kimberley had treated herself to a gorgeous cotton lawn summer dress decorated with small mauve flowers and green leaves on a navy background. It would be ideal for this evening. The sleeves emphasised her slender arms and the V-neck framed her warm, biscuit coloured skin.

After dressing, she brushed and dried her long chestnut hair until it shone and pinned it into an elegant French pleat. A pair of kitten-heeled slip-ons decorated with azure and emerald diamante stones and a pair of matching earrings dressed up the outfit just enough for a special evening at home.

Finally, Kimberley checked the top

drawer of her dressing table where a small package wrapped in elegant silver and black striped paper held a pair of gold cuff links with turquoise stones, the colour of which had reminded her so much of Scott's eyes that she couldn't resist buying them.

All that remained was for her to prepare the salad, put the steaks on a plate, wrap everything in cling film and take it up on to the roof garden ready for their barbecue.

★ ★ ★

The evening was perfect, without a breath of wind. Kimberley had decorated the roof garden the day before, while Scott had been out. The terrace was adorned with two fully-grown Japanese acers in large pots. Crowded on to the branches of each one, Kimberley had carefully hung votive candles in little jewel-coloured glass containers. As she lit each one, the trees' branches came to life in a myriad of colours: royal purple; blood red; amber yellow; malachite green. It looked magical. Once the table was laid with a white linen cloth, champagne flutes, silver candlesticks and a bowl of red roses, Kimberley couldn't help thinking it looked good enough for the cover of Homes And Gardens. She rarely had time nowadays to do anything like this, but an anniversary was such a special day.

An Evening To Remember

Kimberley heard Scott's key in the door, and her heart skipped as she held the rail of the spiral staircase and made her way down to greet him. It was wonderful that, after three years of married life, that the thought of seeing him could still affect her like this.

'Hello, darling. I've had such a day,' Scott's voice called out. As she came down the stairs, he was standing in the lounge, taking small change and his mobile phone out of the pockets of his jacket. He turned, saw her, and stopped in his tracks, saying, 'Wow, you look stunning.'

'Thank you. Not only have I dressed up for you, I have also prepared us a very special dinner,' Kimberley told him.

As she came over to him, he opened his arms and enfolded her in a long, lingering kiss. Kimberley felt her head swim at his embrace, delighting in the sensation of being enclosed in his strong arms. This felt so much like a special anniversary kiss. Her heart filled with the hope that he hadn't forgotten their big day after all.

He released her and took off his jacket, striding back into the hall to hang it on the stand. 'Today was absolutely awesome,' he called out to her, 'and it's so sweet of you to dress up and do a special dinner to celebrate my success.'

Standing alone in the lounge, Kimberley suddenly found it difficult to swallow. Scott thought the dinner was all to do with his business deal! All day, she had been thinking of their anniversary and, unless she was much mistaken, it had barely crossed his mind. She inhaled deeply to try and settle the upset she could feel welling up inside her. Of course it had been an utterly momentous day for him. This deal meant everything; it would be the pinnacle of his career and the gateway to so much success. When she had worked in the office full-time and been the centre of things, she would have moved Heaven and Earth herself to secure such a deal. But now, her priorities were shifting. It seemed his had not.

Kimberley steadied herself. She must get this into perspective. Being a good husband wasn't merely about remembering special days, it was about all the other 364 days in the year; and Scott was normally such an attentive husband. It was only lately things had started to change. A tear escaped from the corner of her eye, but that was selfish, she chided herself. What did it matter if he had forgotten their anniversary? The way he had kissed her just now proved he loved her as much as ever. She wiped the tear away quickly and tried to sound normal. 'So did it go well?' she said.

'It was touch and go for a time,' Scott told her, coming back into the lounge and settling into the sofa. 'I could murder a drink, sweetheart, is there anything cool in the fridge?'

Kimberley managed a smile as she went to the kitchen. In the fridge was the bottle of champagne she had put in to chill. She had chosen it especially because it bore the year of their marriage, the year they had sworn to have and to hold, for better or worse. She ran her finger over the numbers engraved in gold lettering on the label. As she wrapped a tea towel around the icy bottle and took it in to Scott with two champagne flutes, she wondered if this was one of the better or worse times. He had obviously triumphed today, but that was tinged with sadness for her by the fact that his work seemed to have taken precedence over their marriage.

'Champagne, Kimberley? I'm really touched by your confidence in me. Trust you to know we'd have a celebration to toast this evening. Here, let me do that for you.' Scott took the bottle and expertly turned it while holding the cork. A satisfying 'pop' and he was pouring the sparkling liquid into the glasses without even a drip on to the table. His eyes were alight with excitement. 'You know, it's amazing how far we've come. Do you remember when we were students together and I had that awful job as a wine waiter in that two-bit dive that called itself a restaurant and I used to wonder whether we'd ever be able to afford champagne? Well, now my love,' he raised his glass to hers, 'I reckon we might be able to bathe in vintage champagne.'

Their glasses clinked together and Kimberley tried to get over her disappointment. She knew she mustn't spoil this triumph for Scott, so she smiled and asked him to tell her all about it.

As he talked, he was bubbling over with the emotional drama of the negotiations. She listened politely and was genuinely delighted for him, but couldn't help wondering at the excited light in his eyes. She'd seen that sort of look a few times before. Then, uncomfortably, it came to her.

A friend from university days had helped to pay for his tuition by running a poker game. It had seemed extraordinary to her at the time, gambling seemed such an odd way to pay for your education, but her friend was good at it. The only thing was, even when he'd made enough for his tuition, he couldn't stop trying for greater and greater winnings. That same light she now saw disturbingly in Scott's eyes. It was a sort of addiction, although Scott's addiction was for work. He was as high as a kite on his success.

'So you see,' he concluded, 'we nailed the deal. All of us worked together. It was magic!'

Kimberley went over to him as he sat on the sofa sipping his champagne, and ran her fingers through his dark hair. 'I'm really pleased for you, love,' she said. 'Now, do you fancy some dinner?'

'Of course, I've been forgetting

you've spent half the day shopping and cooking. Sorry, sweetheart.' He got up, preparing to follow her up the spiral staircase. 'How was your day?' he asked.

She couldn't mention the anniversary. He would be miserable if he realised he'd forgotten. But, of course, she had other news to tell him. 'Well, actually, I've got some pretty extraordinary news, too. Do you remember my parents talking about Cousin Grace . . . ?' But Kimberley's voice was drowned out by the trilling ring tone on Scott's mobile phone.

Scott pounced on it as if his life depended upon answering the call. 'Joe,' he declared, 'yeah, we got the deal, isn't that fantastic?' In a second it was as if Kimberley wasn't even in the room. As Scott went over the triumphs of the day with Joe, one of his work colleagues, Kimberley walked slowly up the stairs and waited on the rooftop garden in the cool night air. Every now and then snatches of Scott's conversation reached her ears.

'Yeah, of course, it's going to be pretty heavy over the next months . . . You're right, no-one in the team knows the case as well as I do . . . It might even mean the odd night spent sleeping over in the office, you know how pressured these cases can get, but I'm up for it . . . '

By the time Scott had finished his conversation and come up stairs, the steaks were nearly done. As they sat down to eat, Scott relayed to her proudly that Joe was now one of the senior partners and had rung to congratulate him. 'See how much it means to secure business like this? Suddenly, you get known in all the right places! Joe can be a bit scary. His name's Joe Hatcher, but he's known as Mr Hatchet by the juniors because he doesn't suffer fools gladly. I'll have my work cut out trying to please him.'

'Mmm,' Kimberley replied, toying with the salad on her plate. Scott sat back. 'Hey, are you OK? Oh, no,

Kimberley, I'm sorry, I've been neglecting you.' As he reached his hand over and touched hers, for one uplifting moment she thought he'd remembered that this was their anniversary. But then he said, 'didn't you say you had some pretty extraordinary news, too? Cousin Grace or something, wasn't it? I'm sorry, I've been going on and on and not asking you about your day.'

Kimberley smiled weakly. 'Yes, I was starting to tell you. My father's cousin, Grace Drake, has died. We've been left a house, Scott, a house in the country. On the Isle of Wight.'

Scott sat back, all attention on Kimberley now.

'A house? On the Isle of Wight? That's amazing! I've never been there. It's off the coast at Hampshire isn't it?'

'That's right. The only details I have came in a letter from the solicitors today. It's in the office if you want to go and check on what they say about the bequest. I only went to the Isle of Wight a couple of times as a toddler. I've no idea what the island's like now, or the house. Cousin Grace was a bit eccentric by all accounts, crazy about animals, so I imagine the house might be rather old and rickety.'

'Isn't that weird that I was saying to you only this morning that if I secured the Tavistock deal we could afford a cottage in the country? Now, we can afford a decent-sized country house if you sell your Cousin Grace's old wreck.'

Kimberley put down her knife and fork. 'Why would I want to sell it? And I didn't say it was an old wreck.'

'You as much as said she was a bit of a dotty old bird who was crazy about cats and dogs, so I don't suppose maintenance and DIY was exactly her thing. If we sell it and put the money you get from it together with the bonus I'll get from the Tavistock deal, we could afford something classy in Surrey.'

'Why would we want somewhere there?'

'Because it's close to London, of

course. Look honey, I'm going to be more in demand than ever at work now, so I need to be near the office. The Tavistock deal involves a lot of business with their office in America. They operate on a completely different time clock from us, so I may need to go to the office to do teleconferences even at the weekend.'

Scott must have detected the disappointment in Kimberley's face, because he squeezed her hand in an effort at reassurance saying, 'Don't look so downcast. We can get a nice place with a big garden in Surrey, and if need be, all I have to do is hop on a train to get into London. Then, because it's so close I can hop back again to finish off the weekend with you. It'll work out fine.'

'You mean you've worked it all out without even thinking of what I might want.' Kimberley was aware she was being prickly, but she couldn't help herself. 'I have no idea what Cousin Grace's house is like and I'm certainly not going to make any decisions about it until I've seen it. Anyway, don't you think the fact that she left it to me means that we ought to treat her bequest with some respect? She loved that place, she lived there for years, it meant everything to her. I'm sure when she left it to me it was because she decided I was one of the youngest members of the family and that I'd be more likely to do the house up and keep it on.'

'What?' Scott laughed. 'Preserve some old relic we don't want, in memory of someone you didn't even know?'

* * *

Kimberley could feel her cheeks getting redder, and removed her hand from Scott's. If he had been in a more receptive mood and less wrapped up in his own affairs, she would have told him that Cousin Grace hadn't just been keen on animals, but that her house was actually an animal sanctuary, but he'd

43

probably just have laughed at that. And somehow, Kimberley would have felt upset if he'd laughed at what had been her relative's life's work.

'My father and mother knew Grace very well at one time, when they were all a lot younger,' she said. 'I wish I had known her better. I wish we'd made more effort to keep in touch, although Mum says it was Cousin Grace who decided to cut herself off from the world and just have her animals. I have to say, the more I think about it, the more I can see her point. At least animals bring you comfort, whereas contact with people can prove a lot more difficult.'

Kimberley looked at Scott pointedly. 'Anyway, I've arranged to go down to Cousin Grace's solicitors tomorrow, with Mum, to find out exactly what the bequest is all about. Perhaps we can have a more reasonable conversation once we know what all this involves. Until then, I can't see much point in talking about it.'

With that, she picked up the plates, scraping her half-eaten meal on to his empty plate, turned her back on him and set off downstairs. When she got to the kitchen, she immediately felt bad about making a scene. The strawberries and cream she had lovingly bought as homage to their last anniversary sat in bowls, neglected, on the kitchen top. The present she had bought for Scott lay upstairs in the bedroom, ungifted, unopened. This day was turning into a disaster.

Last year, at their picnic on the beach, they had giggled as they dipped the strawberries in cream and sugar and fed them to each other, and spent the rest of the evening curled up together under the stars wrapped in the car blanket, as in tune with each other as two violins. But now, everything had got so complicated, and suddenly they seemed so far apart.

It wouldn't do, though. One thing Kimberley's mother had told her on her wedding day was that it was fatal to any marriage for a couple to go to sleep without making up after a quarrel. And this was still Scott's big day.

Kimberley resolved to go upstairs and apologise and simply forget about the anniversary stuff. What did it matter if he had forgotten? He was busy making plans for their future and she was genuinely pleased for him that his work was going so well. Not to be pleased would be churlish.

She took a tray and put the strawberries, cream, and bowl of icing sugar on it and made her way up to the roof garden. When she got there, Scott had gone. A slight chill had whipped up, but it wasn't that which made Kimberley shiver. It was the thought that perhaps he might have gone out and left her on her own.

Had she really been so nasty to him earlier? Had she totally spoilt his momentous day? She hadn't heard the front door closing, but he could simply have had enough and quietly gone out while she was in the kitchen.

Kimberley stood in the cool air, goose bumps dotting her arms, remembering an incident a couple of weeks ago. They had been due to go to a concert, the tickets were bought and Scott had promised he would come home early to pick her up, particularly as he'd had to work late so many times that week and they had hardly seen each other. Time had worn on and he hadn't appeared. When he phoned her to say he'd been held up at the office, he'd urged her to go on to the concert hall alone and gave his word he would meet her there in time for the start.

She had waited and waited, and not only had he not turned up, he had not phoned her. Then he'd finally arrived.

'I've been waiting for ages Scott, what on earth happened to you?' she had said.

'My counterpart in the States rang and I had to get some papers off to him. It wasn't something that could have waited, Kimberley.'

'But you could have phoned me. It seems to me you've always got time for your workmates, but not for me. Why didn't you give me a ring to tell me you wouldn't make the beginning of the concert? It began fifteen minutes ago.'

'If I'd kept on phoning you it would have taken me even longer to get here. Why on earth didn't you go in on your own? You're not a child, Kimberley.'

'All right, I will. I'm going in now, whether you're coming or not.'

'Well, actually,' he'd said, tearing up his ticket, grabbing her hand and plonking the torn pieces into it, 'I think I'd rather not.' With that he had walked off. Once the concert had finished, he had been waiting outside the concert hall for her, looking cold and dejected, while she was red-eyed and missing him.

They'd made up, but it seemed to Kimberley that, even then, his job was coming between them. Would this be another occasion?

She walked over to the railing around the roof garden and hung on to it, beginning to feel as upset as she had when she had sat at the concert with his empty seat next to her. Dejectedly, she thought of the wasted strawberries and the wasted evening when, unexpectedly, she felt warmth clothe her chilly shoulders and turned to find Scott gently placing her green woollen pashmina around her.

In his hands, he held the post, including the anniversary cards she had meant to put out in the lounge but had forgotten, in her rush to get ready this evening.

'I went to read the letter you had got from the solicitor and I found these. Happy anniversary, darling. I am SO, SO sorry I didn't realise when I got in.' He had wrapped the pashmina around her and stood holding her shoulders, his azure eyes as beautiful as ever. 'Can you believe me when I say I didn't forget totally? It had been on my mind weeks ago. I even bought you a present and a card and hid them away carefully at the back of my sock drawer so you wouldn't find them.'

'You did?'

'I know it's no excuse, but in all the anxiety leading up to my meeting, the date slipped my mind. I thought I remembered that dress from some-where, you look so gorgeous. You wore it on our anniversary last year, didn't you?'

'Yes. I suppose I wanted to recreate that day. It was so lovely, wasn't it?'

'Yes, and now I've spoiled today for you, haven't I?'

'No, Scott.' She laid her head on his chest. 'You haven't spoiled it. I know your work is important and I'm pleased for you.'

'You're what's important to me.'

Kimberley looked up at him, search-ing for the truth, wondering where his priorities really lay. 'I'm sorry darling.' He took her chin in his hand, tilted her face upwards and she felt his lips on hers. Suddenly, everything felt better.

As she felt his arms gently pull her to him, it was as if the old Scott had been away somewhere, but had now come back to her.

* * *

When he released her, she felt so warm it was almost as if she was glowing. 'Wait here,' he said, guiding her gently to a chair. She sat back contentedly, looking at the stars in the bright sky and seeing the lights from the guttering candles glowing pink and blue and green and yellow through the leaves of the acers.

When he came back, he handed her a present and a card. The sentiment inside the card told her she was the best wife in the world, and made her want to cry. She opened the package which was enchantingly done up in pink paper with a red ribbon. Inside was a pad of hand-made notepaper and a gold pen. 'Look at the inscription,' urged Scott.

Engraved on the pen lid was the date

of their wedding and a message saying, 'To Kimberley. I love you more each day. Scott.'

How could she ever have doubted him?

First Sight Of The Sanctuary

When Kimberley awoke the next morning, she saw a yellow Post-it placed on Scott's pillow. 'Love you darling, have a good day and say hi to your mum.'

Kimberley looked at her alarm clock. It was still only 7 a.m. Scott must have gone well before sunrise. She sighed and picked up his gift, the elegant, slender gold pen, twirling it in the early morning sunshine and looking at the beams reflecting back the inscription. Over on Scott's bedside table was her present to him, the opened box minus his cufflinks which he had been so pleased with and must have worn this morning.

She missed Scott so much when he wasn't here. Their times together were the most precious moments she had. One of the reasons they had stretched themselves to the limit buying this expensive flat in the centre of London was so that they could be near work and have some time together in the mornings. But lately, even their cosy breakfasts together had been abandoned when Scott wanted to get to the office early.

★   ★   ★

Kimberley carefully hung up her anniversary dress, as she had now come to think of it, before she went in to shower. She had arranged to meet her mother at Waterloo station to catch the 9.14 train.

As she towel-dried her hair in the large bathroom, luxuriating in the spotlit atmosphere with the black marble floor and the Italian white marble walls, Kimberley wondered what Cousin Grace's house would be like. They had become so used to luxury and easy living here. Everything in the flat had been created by designers and it had been all ready to move in, so they hadn't had to do a thing.

Kimberley took out her black skinny jeans which were comfortable but stylish and teamed them with a plain white long sleeved T-shirt. Together with flat gold pump shoes, her outfit looked casual but smart.

As she made her usual breakfast of muesli and fresh mango, she felt a lightness of heart which was heightened by sitting on her balcony breakfasting in the sunshine listening to the bustle of the busy streets of London below. She'd always loved fresh air and crisp bright mornings like this, but although she and Scott often walked in the city, it wasn't quite the same as walking by the sea.

Kimberley tried to dredge up her few hazy memories of Cousin Grace's, but could only recall that it was very near the sea.

Glancing at her watch, she thought she would have just enough time to check over her e-mails before setting off for Waterloo. As she fired up the computer, Kimberley could feel her stress levels beginning to rise. It was always like this. As soon as she started to relax, she would remember something which had to be done. In this age of e-mailing, mobile phones, BlackBerrys and the like, her life was dominated by her work almost twenty-four hours a day. Even on a day off like this, she was compelled, as now, to keep up with work. People expected instant replies and seemed to operate around the clock, and so must she.

As the computer clicked and whirred into life, Kimberley tapped her foot. When she had seen the doctor about her inability to have a baby, he had warned her that she must learn to relax. She felt her blood pressure rising now, when she saw there were twenty messages in her inbox, and she quickly dashed off holding replies to all of them.

Organised as she was, there was

simply too much work to do. Always. She hastily shut down the computer, telling herself everything else could wait, and grabbed her briefcase, checking that she had her mobile. She thrust a file of papers and a couple of contracts in her briefcase. She never went anywhere without some written work to do in case she had the time while travelling. Time was too precious to waste.

Taking a last look at herself in the hallway mirror, Kimberley put on her new Zara mackintosh which belted at the waist, grabbed her sunglasses and set off.

* * *

Waterloo station was teeming, as usual. Sharply suited men strode by with newspapers tucked under their arms, lost-looking tourists clustered by their suitcases, and brisk city girls with crisp shirts and glossy hair clicked by in their high heels as Kimberley waited under the station clock.

When she heard a tuneful 'whoo-oo' and saw a hand waving through the crowd, Kimberley went to greet her mother. Mrs Celia Drake kissed her daughter on the cheek and received a hug in return.

'Hello, darling. Do you think we've got enough time to grab a coffee before getting on the train?'

'Of course, Mum. And thank you so much for coming today.'

'It's no trouble, sweetheart. Actually, it's a bit of an adventure for me. It's just a shame it's a sad event that's brought it all about.'

They stood in the queue at the AMT coffee cabin and decided to treat themselves. Kimberley elected to have a chocolate croissant and her favourite creamy white latte, while Celia went for a large cappuccino and an almond croissant. All were carefully placed in a small paper carrier by the jovial Italian waiter who served them.

* ★ ★

58

At that time of day, the trains going out of London weren't at all crowded. They found themselves seats and spread out over four which had a table between them. Kimberley quickly sent a text message to Scott to let him know she had met up with her mother and to send her love. Before he got so busy, they would regularly send texts during the day, just a little something to brighten up their working lives.

Kimberley put her phone back in her bag, hoping for it to beep with a message from him soon, and then she and Celia tucked into their croissants and sipped their coffee. Once they had finished, Celia opened her handbag. 'I've brought some photographs of Cousin Grace and The Sanctuary that I dug out last night.'

'Great. Maybe they'll jog my memory of the place.'

'This was a holiday we had staying in one of the cottages near Cousin Grace's place, or, should I say, your place.'

'That sounds so strange. I barely

remember any of it, but, looking at these photos, the area looks very beautiful.'

'It is, or rather, it was. Goodness knows what it's like now. Things change so much these days with all the development that goes on, particularly in seaside places. But I have a feeling that not much changes in Highview Cove, which is where The Sanctuary is.'

As the train trundled out of the station and made its way past tightly packed flats and houses, Kimberley examined the photos, some in colour, some in black and white. They showed a picturesque bay with about fifteen small houses nestling in the lee of a hill, and one, much larger, Victorian house about halfway up. Some steep steps at either end of the bay led to it.

'I remember a bit now,' Kimberley said, 'I certainly remember having to walk up and down a lot of steps.'

'That's right, Highview Cove can't be reached by car. There's a small parking place at the top of the cliff, but apart from approaching by boat, there's no way of reaching the houses in the bay other than by walking. Now I think about it, it's a daft place to even contemplate having an animal sanctuary. But Grace was so caring and so happy to be woken up at all hours of the day and night with people bringing in needy animals. And I suppose, away from cars and traffic, it's the perfect place for animals to recover.'

Next, Kimberley turned to a photograph of Cousin Grace. 'She was a really good-looking woman wasn't she, if a little severe. Did she ever marry?'

'No. I know she wanted to. She loved children as much as her animals. She was certainly very smitten with you. But it didn't happen. For some people, however much they plan or want something, their life just doesn't take that path.'

Kimberley felt a jolt deep inside. Her mother knew she and Scott had been trying for a baby, but she didn't know how desperate they were getting and how nothing they did seemed to bring the longed-for pregnancy about. Poor Cousin Grace. Kimberley held the photograph in her hand and touched the strong features and the open smile. Had she, too, felt that aching in her heart as she grew older and there was no prospect of a family in sight?

Kimberley looked up to find her mother studying her. 'Kimberley darling, I hope you don't mind me saying this, but you look very thin. I really wish you'd eat more. It's not as if you don't like food. I've never seen anyone demolish a chocolate croissant as quickly as that. Do you eat properly while you're working?'

Kimberley blushed, her mother always could find her out. 'Sometimes I just forget. Working from home is good, I find it a lot less stressful than being in the office, but I sometimes feel I have to work even harder to prove myself.'

'What do you mean?'

'Some people see home working as a soft option and I like to prove they're wrong, that I can produce just as much, if not more.'

'That's not good, Kimberley. No wonder you're so skinny. You and Scott will burn yourselves out. When do you ever have time for anything other than work?'

Kimberley waved Celia's comments away, but she couldn't help dwelling on them. Work had seemed to take over. Gradually, without her and Scott noticing, it had stolen more and more of their precious young married life.

* * *

As they pulled into Alton station, Kimberley told her mother that they were to be met by Mark Steyning, the solicitor. Getting off the train, Kimberley guessed that the studious looking man with dark suit, glasses and concerned expression, was Mark Steyning, even before he tentatively waved at them. She supposed him to be about the same age as Scott, but he looked older, with his conservative haircut and plain white shirt.

'Your train was bang on time,' Mark Steyning said, opening the door of his top-of-the-range Volvo.

'It's very kind of you to meet us like this,' Kimberley said.

'No problem. It just makes things easier for everyone,' Mark said, as he eased the car into the traffic.

When they reached the mock Tudor building in which Mitchellson, Steyning and Co had their offices, he showed them into a comfortable mahogany-lined office. There were tall black leather winged armchairs for visitors set in front of a large mahogany desk, neat and uncluttered apart from a bulging green file marked, 'Drake'. Kimberley and Celia made themselves comfortable while Mark's secretary brought them coffees.

'I suppose you must find Alton a bit quieter than London, Mrs Wright,' Mark Steyning said, as he seated himself at the desk.

'A bit, and please call me Kimberley.'

'Well, if you think Alton's quiet, then Highview Cove will seem a world away,' Mark said. 'But I'm jumping the gun, Mrs Wright, I mean, Kimberley. I'll begin by telling you that Mitchellson, Steyning and Co has managed Grace Drake's business for many years. I met Miss Drake myself on quite a few occasions and found her to be a delightful person. Your father's cousin was very easy to do business with and very committed to her cause. I always used to go and see her at The Sanctuary. She preferred it that way and I have to say it was by far one of my most pleasurable duties.'

Kimberley thought Mark Steyning looked rather sad at having lost Cousin Grace and she warmed to him, knowing many London lawyers who never had any time to spend with their clients beyond what was strictly necessary for business.

Opening the file, Mark turned to a flagged document. 'Now, to come to

Grace Drake's will. As I said in my letter, she has bequeathed her house, The Sanctuary, to you, Kimberley. I also said that the bequest wasn't entirely straightforward, and this is what we have come here to discuss.'

'You mean that there were conditions to the bequest,' stated Kimberley.

'That's right. In a nutshell, and doing away with all the whys and the wherefores in the will, which I'm sure you know, as a lawyer, Kimberley, can be a bit ponderous, well, in a nutshell, your Cousin Grace has left the house to you on the condition that you continue to run it as an animal sanctuary.'

'Oh,' Kimberley felt like a skater whizzing along on the ice who suddenly slips and falls over. 'But I don't know anything about running an animal sanctuary. I don't even own a pet. Besides, I have a job already, and a very good one. Is there anybody running the sanctuary at present? I mean, has it all been continued in some way since Cousin Grace's death?'

'There is a lady who lives in Highview Cove, a Mrs Florence Wise, who has worked with your Cousin Grace for many years and who is still employed by her estate. I understand Mrs Wise has two young daughters who also work at The Sanctuary on a voluntary basis. Everything has been going on there as normal, your Cousin Grace was keen to ensure that the animals who are already under the care of The Sanctuary are not disrupted and also that the local people can still bring creatures in knowing they will be looked after. The will stipulates that Florence Wise's salary should be paid for another three years at least, with regular increments.'

'Well, that's a relief.' Kimberley realised she had been holding her shoulders taut at the news and visibly dropped them to relax a little. Her life was already full with her busy work as a solicitor and she wasn't sure that she or Scott could cope with any disruption at present. 'That's simple then; this lady,

Mrs Wise I think you said, of course should continue to run The Sanctuary and then everyone will be happy. I have no idea what I might do with the property, anyway, I've barely had a chance to think about it.' Although Scott has, she could have added, thinking back to her husband urging her to sell it.

'I'm afraid it's not quite as simple as that,' Mark Steyning said.

'What do you mean?' Kimberley's mother asked and put her hand on Kimberley's. She could always tell when her daughter was stressed or worried and all the signs were evident now.

As she felt her daughter's skinny wrists, Celia was concerned that there was just a bit too much going on in Kimberley's life and also that perhaps things at home weren't as rosy as they could be. She had waited all the journey down for Kimberley to talk about her anniversary the day before. She and Scott had always made a big thing of their anniversaries. Even before they married, they'd always celebrated the day they'd met with trips away or evenings out somewhere special. The fact that Kimberley hadn't said a thing about yesterday concerned Celia.

'What I mean, Celia,' Mark continued, 'is that your Cousin Grace made a very clear stipulation that Kimberley was to spend at least two days of every week running The Sanctuary, on site, herself. Furthermore, that this attendance, in person, should continue for at least a year before Kimberley would be entitled to inherit the house. She was very clear in her stipulation that Kimberley's attendance should span fifty-two unbroken weeks, and it should not matter whether it was Christmas or some other holiday or whether there was illness or business issues.'

'Kimberley should, in order to inherit, spend two days of every week, continuously, for a whole year, working at The Sanctuary.'

'B . . . but,' Kimberley stuttered, 'I, well, I simply can't. I have too many commitments. I simply don't have time at the weekends, I often do my best work then . . . '

'You work at the weekends?' Celia interrupted.

She was shocked. Kimberley had never told her that, and Kimberley was now looking just as she had used to as a little girl when she'd been caught out eating too many doughnuts, denying she'd had another when the jammy evidence was clear.

'Not every weekend,' Kimberley moved into damage limitation mode. 'But it has to be done sometimes, Mum. People want contracts turned around in 24 hours, that's just how it is. Isn't that so, Mark?'

Mark Steyning coughed slightly uneasily. 'I'm afraid we don't do things quite like that here, I have to say. We have our busy moments, but this is a family firm and that means family has as much importance as business. As soon as I finish on a Friday at 6 p.m., I don't even think about work until Monday morning.'

'I'm sure your wife and children appreciate that. That's the only way to keep married life going,' Celia said, looking pointedly at Kimberley.

'Sadly, I don't have a wife or children,' Mark Steyning said, 'but I do have brothers and sisters who've given me nieces and nephews with whom I love spending time.

'Now, perhaps I can do something to help. I can see that this news hasn't been exactly welcome. Legacies and bequests often mean change, and that can be difficult. I anticipated that this might be hard to cope with, which is why I offered you a morning appointment. I'm aware that you, Celia, haven't visited the property for many years and that you, Kimberley, won't even remember it, you were so young when you first went there. So, if you're at all interested, I would be happy to take you there today. We can drive down to Lymington and get the ferry over. We'd be there in enough time to view The Sanctuary and have a late lunch before coming back here.'

'It's very short notice,' Kimberley said. She'd anticipated getting back home in time to do some work. Now, she probably wouldn't get back home until late evening. She wanted to check with Scott, but she'd been waiting for him to reply to her text and nothing had come through. 'Could I make a quick phone call?' she said.

'Certainly,' said Mark. 'While you're doing that, I'll ask my secretary to phone Florence Wise and check that she's about. If we do go, it would be useful if you could meet her.'

Discreetly, Mark left the room and Kimberley dialled Scott on her mobile. His mobile didn't answer so she dialled the office. She got through to Scott's secretary, Delia. 'I'm sorry,' Delia said, in her breathy, little girl voice, 'Scott's been incredibly busy today, he hasn't stopped. And now he's out with Joe and some clients. I'll ask him to give you a ring, though, Kimberley.'

He could have replied to my text,

thought Kimberley. It only took a matter of seconds to tap in a message. Then again, it was unprofessional if you were with clients to be constantly looking at your mobile. In a split second she decided to take Mark Steyning up on his offer. After all, she and her mother had come this far and she was available on her mobile for clients, so if any of them needed her desperately, she could speak to them, even from the Isle of Wight.

'Let's go then, shall we?' she said, trying to keep her voice light as Mark Steyning came back into the room.

'Good,' Mark smiled. 'I have to confess that I'm always looking for any excuse to visit Highview Cove. It really is a superb spot.'

★ ★ ★

As they got into Mark's car and headed out towards the M3, Kimberley opened her briefcase and took out some paperwork. It wouldn't do to waste any time and they had an hour's journey to kill. Celia looked over to Kimberley and shook her head. 'There was a time, Kimberley, when you would have had a magazine or something a bit lighter than work to pass the time. When did you last read a novel?'

'I do read, Mum.' She racked her brains but couldn't actually remember the last time she had read for pleasure. It must have been on her holiday last year, certainly too long ago to remember. 'It's just that these need doing and I hadn't planned on a whole day out.'

* * *

As Celia chatted amiably to Mark Steyning, Kimberley found she couldn't keep her concentration on the document in front of her. The words and letters seemed to swim unconnected in front of her vision, her mind was so absorbed with Mark's news. Why on earth would Cousin Grace have imposed such a draconian condition in her will?

Kimberley could understand her relative being thoroughly involved in The Sanctuary and her animals. But if she'd kept on Florence Wise, and presumably that included the help of her two daughters, then why hadn't Grace just stipulated that Kimberley wasn't allowed to sell the property for a period of time? Why would she, in effect, make Kimberley traipse all the way down here, every single week, in person? It certainly wasn't so that Kimberley could bring her knowledge and expertise to The Sanctuary. She knew next to nothing about animals and, apart from probably being younger than Mrs Wise and therefore perhaps a bit more physically able, Kimberley felt that she would be very little use.

Kimberley chewed the end of her pen, a habit she often indulged in when she was worried, then remembered it was the gold pen Scott had given her. She looked again at the inscription, then looked at her mobile. Still not even a simple message to say Hi. Kimberley felt hurt. Scott knew where she was going today, knew it was important to her. Okay, it was family stuff rather than work, but she would really have loved to have talked to him about it.

Finally, Kimberley forced herself to concentrate on her papers and managed to clear one or two documents before they got to the ferry. Mark parked the car, and they were just in time to make the hourly crossing which, thankfully, was calm and clear.

'I must congratulate you on being so organised, Mark,' Kimberley said, as they walked off the ferry and settled into the taxi which Mark had waiting for them.

'I have to confess, it's not entirely selfless. I think I said I always enjoyed coming over here to see your Cousin Grace. I liked both her, and the island. Once you get to know it, it can exercise a sort of pull on your emotions, particularly Highview Cove. The area has its own micro-climate, so it's warm much of the year, and receives far more sunshine than lots of other places.'

As they couldn't drive right into Highview Cove, Mark paid the driver in the small car park at the top of the cliff, and settled for the taxi to come back in around three hours' time . . . Kimberley couldn't help thinking that that was an awfully long time to spend looking at one house, and glanced at her watch. If they were going to have lunch somewhere afterwards, goodness knew when she was going to get back.

Surely, there wouldn't be anywhere down here to have lunch, she thought, peering over the cliff. But, as they made their way down the narrow winding steps with bushes at either side, Highview Cove began to open out to them as the picture on a fan would as it is slowly opened. Kimberley glanced at the backs of the gardens of the fifteen or so houses which were nestled in the cove. As they came closer to the bottom of the cliff, they began to hear and glimpse tiny snatches of the sea until, finally, at the end of the steps they came out into Highview Cove and it was presented before them in all its glory.

Kimberley took it all in. 'Why, Mum, it's absolutely glorious. Why didn't you tell me it was so fantastically beautiful?'

'Well, darling, to us it was just another little holiday place. There were lots of quiet, quaint places then. It's only recently, with all the development that goes on, that places have lost their character, but Highview Cove is certainly not one of them.'

'It certainly isn't,' Mark said, as they stood on the wide path which wound around the cove. 'There's even a fisherman here still. See that house there, the one painted blue and white with the lobster pots and nets in the garden? Well, that's his. You can buy lobster from him.'

'I didn't know places like this still existed.' Kimberley was charmed as they looked around at the little cottages which seemed to hug the bottom of the cliff like puppies sitting at the feet of their mother.

Mark smiled. 'The coastal path going away off up the cliff and over those fields leads to Rantnor, which is a nice town where you can get a great pub lunch. It's just about twenty minutes bracing walk over the cliffs. There are all the shops anyone could want in Rantnor and it's a fabulous way to get fit, walking over there to get supplies and then back again. But, to the right here,' he pointed to the end of the cove, 'after that last house ends, the seafront path ends, which is why there is no traffic and why it's so superbly peaceful. My favourite time here is actually in the winter because the only people around are those who live here. In the summer, lots of holidaymakers come just to enjoy the small beachside café over there, where you can get some of the best crab sandwiches on the island.'

Kimberley's eyes feasted on the wide azure sea, the endless blue sky, the ochre sand where a child ran up and down with a kite, and where tiny rowing boats lay dancing on the water.

It was like a child's picture book. 'And there is your Cousin Grace's house. Or should I say, Kimberley, if you decide to keep it, your house.'

* * *

Kimberley shielded her eyes from the dazzling sunlight, and looked left to where Mark was pointing. There, half way up a small hill, was a wooden gate at the foot of a set of steps. At the top of the steps stood a large detached Victorian house, the last house before the wide path which led to Rantnor down the coast.

The Sanctuary, slightly raised above the little cottages, looked like a grandmother benignly watching over her children. On three sides, it had the most wonderful sea views — from the front, directly out over Highview Cove and out to sea, from the left, it looked east to where the sun rose, and from the right, it looked west to where the sun would set. All three sides of the house had large picture windows and balconies. Whoever built it must have fallen in love with the sea and every phase of its timeless existence. And, as she looked at the old house in its perfect position, Kimberley found herself losing her heart to its charms.

'Shall we go and look inside?' Mark went up to the wooden gate, unfastened the catch and beckoned to them to follow him.

As they started to make their way up the many steps they suddenly heard a loud noise, like a heavy gate with very rusty hinges being opened and closed. Then, out of the blue, running down the hill as fast as his stubby legs would carry him, came a donkey. He came bounding up to them, and allowed Kimberley and Celia to stroke his long brown ears and apologise to him for having nothing to give him to eat.

'Oh, Donkey, you're gorgeous,' laughed Kimberley feeling the coarse dusty fur beneath her fingers. 'What's his name?' she asked Mark.

'That is Sigmund.'

'Sigmund?'

'Yup, named by your Cousin Grace after Sigmund Freud because she reckoned that far from being dim, donkeys were very intuitive creatures and knew exactly what everybody was thinking. He seems to have been here forever and Grace always reckoned that that was the reason why she'd never needed a front doorbell, because Sigmund brays like an Isle of Wight ferry every time he sees someone coming up the steps.'

Reluctantly, they left Sigmund and carried on up to the front door. From this elevated position, the whole of the bay lay before them and as they stood, Kimberley found herself delighting in the smell of the sea and the sound of nothing but the seagulls dipping and rising above them and the waves below kissing the shore. The whole place was so far away from the flat in London. There, she could only see buildings and streets and the roar of traffic was ever present.

'The house is a little ramshackle isn't it?' said Celia, picking at a piece of flaking paint.

'I wouldn't say it was ramshackle,' Kimberley stated, 'just lived in.' As she said the words, Kimberley thought she saw a smile across Mark Steyning's face. It was obvious to her that he recognised all the plus points of The Sanctuary and was pleased she was discovering them. 'It's delightful,' she said.

'It's a bit of a mess if you ask me,' said Celia.

'Oh, Mum, it's not a mess, just very individual.'

They strolled into a huge lounge which had a bay window leading on to a balcony looking over the sea. The floor had a big wine coloured carpet, but you could hardly make it out for all the rugs sitting on top of it. Each one in its own right was lovely, Persian, probably, but they could have done with some cleaning, Kimberley thought.

At the window, the curtains were homely rather than smart, having been made up of patches of all sorts of different materials. Similarly, the chair covers were made up of different coloured patches of multi-coloured plain velvet. Kimberley smiled as she wondered whether there was a single thing in this house that matched.

As they went into the kitchen at the back of the house, Kimberley was beginning to get a picture of her Cousin Grace.

In the kitchen, there stood a large dresser full of cups and saucers, but not one single cup matched one single saucer. They were all a delightful hotch-potch of flowery, plain, pastel, gold-rimmed, slim and elegant, small and dumpy cups in front of more varieties of saucer than Kimberley had ever seen in one place.

'I don't think decorating was quite Grace's thing,' Celia said, looking at the yellowing walls which had probably once been white.

'It just needs a bit of freshening up.'

'When did you last do any decorating?'

'I don't actually remember,' said Kimberley, thinking back to her pristine, clinical flat. She loved that flat for its simplicity and the ease of living there. But this house had character oozing out of every nook and cranny. It was comfortable and homely and perfectly right for a house by the sea.

★ ★ ★

Mark led them upstairs and Kimberley gasped when she saw the master bedroom. Each wall was painted a different colour blue, and on a plate rack, which ran around the top of the room, were row after row of models of boats. Over by one wall was a large scrubbed wooden table with a beautiful display of shells and pieces of driftwood bleached by the sun. Mark walked over to the French windows, opening them to let the sun and the air suffuse the room.

The bed, which had a beautiful blue and white patchwork quilt, was positioned with its feet to the ocean and Kimberley could imagine the sheer joy of lying here looking out over the sea and listening to the waves. It was Heaven, Paradise.

Again, the curtains needed a good wash and the rugs could have done with a thorough beating and a shampoo, but the room itself was delightful.

'Shall we go and see the animals?' Mark led them back down to the kitchen and through the back door.

The back of the house was dwarfed by the hill, but this, Mark explained, had been carefully thought out by Cousin Grace as the best place for the recuperation sheds, as they were protected from the worst of the elements. Being warmer in winter as it was sheltered from the breeze by the house and cooler in the summer as much of it was in the shade, made the area ideal for convalescing animals. And there, in modern pens, were a multitude of different creatures all looking very much at home.

There was a large pen with three swans in it, a smaller one with a gull with a broken wing. Then there was a pen where they could just glimpse a hedgehog rolled up asleep in a bundle of straw and another which held a large brown mottled rabbit who was demolishing a pile of leaves. A little further on, on the side of the hill, they saw goats, a sheep and a miniature Shetland pony.

'Grace used to take in any kind of animal, domestic or wild, anything that was abandoned, unwanted or injured, and she had a whole network of sanctuaries and wildlife centres which she knew around the country where she would send animals if she couldn't care for them herself.'

'So this animal population is constantly changing?' Kimberley was intrigued at the variety of animals as she knelt down, stroking the soft fur of the rabbit.

'That's right. One week I'd come here and find she had loads of birds in, usually after a storm or some bad weather. Then, most usually after Christmas, she'd have a sudden influx of domestic pets, dogs and cats and guinea pigs, which people had abandoned. This place is a bit like an orphanage really, and the animals were her children. She often used to say so herself.'

'How on earth did Cousin Grace know how to treat the animals?'

'She didn't do it entirely on her own. There's a vet at the top of the hill, within walking distance, with whom she had an excellent relationship, who would help to treat the animals or advise Grace on how to handle them. Don't let the slightly unkempt feel of the house fool you. Grace was a very methodical woman and she liked to be independent. She kept countless journals, all catalogued and cross-referenced, which she would write up at the end of each day. They're in the bookcases lining the walls of the lounge. Quite frankly, she had almost as much knowledge as your average vet. She'd keep notes and pencil drawings to remind her of how she'd treated her various charges and brought them back to health. She really was a remarkable woman.'

'I'm beginning to see that more and more.' The more Kimberley heard about how much love and attention Cousin Grace had put into her life's work and the more time she spent in this quirky, lived-in home, the more she felt drawn to it. One thing which puzzled her was why Cousin Grace hadn't felt more able to be friendly with her own family. When Kimberley had first heard about the bequest and heard her mother talk briefly about their elderly relative, she got the impression that Grace Drake had been a cold, hard woman, who didn't like the company of people and had instead turned to animals. But from what Mark was saying, she wasn't like that at all.

She had good relations with Florence Wise, who Mark had said they were shortly to meet, and with Mrs Wise's two daughters, who obviously liked working here so much they did it for free. Furthermore, Cousin Grace had been so likeable and persuasive, that the local vet, who was no doubt very busy, did her favours.

And by all accounts, Grace had been such a pleasant person to spend time with, that Mark Steyning, a young man with a busy job, tried to get over here to spend time in The Sanctuary as much as possible. Why then, had relations become so frosty with members of Grace's own family? There was obviously something Celia wasn't telling Kimberley and she resolved to quiz her mother on the journey back.

★ ★ ★

As they were standing petting the Shetland pony, Kimberley realised she had left her briefcase upstairs and excused herself to go and get it.

When she got up to Cousin Grace's bedroom, she already felt quite proprietorial about the old house and when she found the French windows still open, and the wind rising from the sea, she went to close them.

As she did, there was a loud braying from Sigmund and she looked out to see a slender young girl with flowing blonde hair greeting the donkey, who seemed to know her. The girl, who was dressed in low hipped jeans and a red hoody with writing like graffiti all over it, held out portions of carrot which she had carefully sliced lengthways. As Kimberley shut the windows and locked them quietly so as not to disturb the young visitor, she saw the girl wrap her arms around the donkey's neck and lean her head on his brown fur. He looked perfectly at ease. She kissed his neck and broke off for a rummage around in her bag for the last few carrots.

Kimberley was intrigued by the girl,

who was beautiful in a gawky, teenager way. She was struck by how much care the girl was showing the donkey as he chomped his carrots. Carefully Kimberley went downstairs and opened the front door, wondering whether the girl knew there were other animals and if she'd like to see the Shetland pony. But as Kimberley made her way down the steps, the girl suddenly saw her and her body language changed instantly. Her shoulders hunched and she looked terrified, as if she had been caught out doing something wrong.

'Hello,' said Kimberley. But the girl turned tail and ran down the steps.

'Don't be scared,' called out Kimberley, 'you haven't done anything wrong. What's your name?' But the girl didn't answer. She had shot down the steps and was now at the gate, fumbling with the catch and panicking in a way Kimberley found quite odd. The girl was so scared that Kimberley saw her cut her hand on the gate. 'You've hurt yourself. Let me look at that.'

But the girl took no notice and, finally getting the lock undone, threw the gate open and fled off down the seafront path so fast that sand and pebbles flew up. She tore past the first houses in Highview Cove and then disappeared into one of the end cottages, leaving Kimberley standing mystified at the gate.

Kimberley Makes a Decision

'Is everything OK?' Mark was standing at the doorstep with a questioning look on his face.

'It's fine,' Kimberley said, as she fastened the gate. 'When are we going to meet Florence Wise?' Maybe that lady would have some idea of who the young girl was and why she had run away like a scared cat, Kimberley thought.

'I hope it's OK, but I've asked Florence to meet us down by the café on the seafront. We can chat over crab sandwiches.'

'That sounds great.'

The day was turning out to be far more interesting and pleasant than Kimberley had imagined, she thought, as they strolled along the sea path with the cove spread out in front of them. The sun here seemed so much warmer than in the city and the colours so much brighter and vibrant. Kimberley had heard of artists setting up colonies in places like Cornwall because of the clean sea air and the special quality of the light, and now she could see why.

Kimberley and Celia sat outside at one of the tables set out on the café's veranda and looked quietly at the rolling sea while Mark went in and greeted the owners, who he obviously knew well.

When they heard Mark say, 'Ah, Florence, come and meet my new friends,' both Kimberley and Celia got up to see a very rounded lady in her forties who held out an instantly welcoming hand which was accompanied by a smile as warm as cakes from the oven.

'Any relatives of Grace Drake are friends of mine.' She shook their hands and then looked suddenly sad. 'I'm so sorry for your loss. Grace was a great friend as well as my employer. I hardly felt I worked *for* her as such. We worked together, her and I, and I loved it so much she had to order me out sometimes, tell me to go home, I was that happy at The Sanctuary.'

They chatted easily about the animals and the area, with Florence telling them that Highview Cove was a wonderful little community all on its own. In her friendly, jovial way, she gave them a run down of all the permanent residents and the characters who lived in the Cove, while Mark went off to get them drinks and order some lunch.

Sitting on the café's veranda, right at the end of the line of cottages, they could see every residence spread out before them, with The Sanctuary sitting at the end of the cove.

'That one, that pink cottage, who lives there?' asked Kimberley, nodding her thanks to Mark, who had just delivered steaming hot mugs of tea and then gone to fetch the sandwiches. If anyone would know who the mysterious teenager was who had run away from her, Florence Wise would, Kimberley reasoned.

'That's a holiday cottage, although it's been on quite a long let now, about three months all through the winter, in fact,' Florence told Kimberley. 'There's a rather good-looking chap living there, well, he would be if he tidied himself up a bit. Could do with smiling on occasions, too. He looks a bit like a gypsy, all black wavy hair and dark eyes. But his daughter is as blonde as a palomino's mane, beautiful child to look at but strange, very strange. Built very tall he is and must be fit as a fiddle. I see him go running most mornings right over the cliffs and back again. He doesn't seem to work.' Florence snorted with disapproval. 'How anybody gets by without working I don't know, especially with a teenage daughter to look after. I haven't seen her going off to school, neither, which seems wrong to me.'

'You said she was strange. What do you mean by that?' Kimberley asked.

'Never talks. Never.' Florence sat back and folded her arms as if this omission was some sort of personal insult to her. 'Rudeness I'd say it is, plain rudeness. I wouldn't have it in my own daughters, no way. I've seen her fussing around Sigismund a couple of times.'

'Sigismund?' Celia, looking completely lost, said in an aside to Kimberley.

'Sigmund, the donkey.'

'Oh.'

★ ★ ★

It was clear once Florence Wise was up and running, nothing would stop her, ' . . . not that I mind her petting Sigismund, he loves it, that silly old creature, he'll take any amount of stroking and he comes right up to the fence, but it's a bit difficult for her to reach him that way, so one day I saw her and said, come in, open the gate and come in, I always like to be friendly, me. But d'you know what she did, she just turned and ran like I'd ticked her off or something.

'Perhaps her dad's strict with her, ticks her of an' stuff, I don't know. I shouldn't be surprised. He looks very sour that one, never smiles. Never. Poor kiddie, fancy having to live with that, an' no mother around neither, not that I've seen.'

'Who is this girl?' asked Celia, as Mark arrived back with sandwiches stuffed with fresh crab and lettuce. As they tucked in, Kimberley related how she had briefly met the girl and said that her experience was very similar to Florence's.

★ ★ ★

As Kimberley sat listening to the chatter and finishing off her sandwich, she gazed over the scene in front of her and then thought back to her office in the quiet flat in the middle of a busy city where she spent her days alone, toiling over mountains of paper. Suddenly, her work seemed like so many words which meant nothing. Some of her clients she had never even met, never even — and the thought jolted her like an electric shock — spoken to. She got written instructions, pored over her computer, and sent off replies. E-mails flitted back and forth but they were like so much empty techno traffic. Was that what her work consisted of, a soulless robotic concentration on contracts, in a lonely office with sterile text books, teasing out points of law?

The girl and the animals, Florence and the lived-in old house, the colours, the sheer beauty and emotional vibrance of this lively community had all touched Kimberley's heart in a way that her work never had. In that second, she made her decision, more with her heart than her head, that she could not let The Sanctuary go. She would not sell it, she would keep it. She would keep on this amiable rounded woman sitting in front of her chatting animatedly. She would somehow ensure that all the animals were loved and cared for until she could find them good homes. She would whirl through The Sanctuary like a new brush and would shake the dust off the carpets, shampoo the colour back into them, paint the walls and make it fresh and new like this beautiful fresh new day. And if she and Scott didn't have children, she thought, this place and the animals would help her over that sadness.

But what would Scott think?

Excusing herself, Kimberley walked to the end of the veranda with her phone and dialled Scott's mobile. There was the same message she had heard a thousand times when she'd tried to phone him and he'd been busy. So she simply left a message to say she loved him and decided that if he wasn't there to consult, she'd just have to make her own decisions.

Kimberley Learns About Grace

'But darling, surely you should have consulted Scott.' Celia regarded her daughter sitting opposite her on the train racing back to London, concern etched into her fine features. Kimberley had signed the papers and it was all arranged with Mark Steyning that she would accept the bequest and with it, the obligation to stay at The Sanctuary two days out of every week.

'Mum, how can I consult Scott if he's never there to talk to?' Kimberley said.

Celia sighed. That was just one of the things she was worried about. Kimberley had, for once, eaten her lunch with gusto, and Celia had been pleased to see how animatedly she had chattered as she had put away a large slice of coffee and walnut cake. Celia had always worried about how Kimberley went off her food when she had problems, and she could see now, in her daughter's cheekbones which were more prominent than usual, signs that Kimberley had been going through difficult times. Quite often when Celia had called over the last six months, Scott had been working — early morning, late evening, it didn't matter when Celia phoned, there was no Scott around, and she worried about her daughter spending too much time alone in her flat, working.

'What did he think about you taking on The Sanctuary in the first place?' she asked now.

'He wanted to sell it.'

'Oh. To be honest, I thought you'd do that. How on earth will you manage to keep up with your work and spend two days of every week down there?'

'Mum,' Kimberley looked determined and reminded Celia of the bold, focused little girl who had turned into the beautiful woman sitting in front of her. 'How could you think of my selling The Sanctuary after what we saw today? Cousin Grace was so committed to her work and it simply wouldn't seem right to just rub it all out without even trying to give it a go.'

'But what . . . well, what would happen, darling, if . . . if you ever got pregnant?'

Kimberley was silent as she stared out of the window.

'I'm sorry to be so blunt, darling, and I know it's a very sore subject but I know you'd never give up your work, even if you did have a child. So how on earth could you manage two homes, one a working animal sanctuary, as well as being a new mother?'

'Oh, Mum, please don't.'

'Kimberley, what is it?' As Celia watched her daughter, she saw her lovely face crumple and tears start to brim over. Celia got up from her seat and went to sit next to her daughter, cradling her head on her shoulder. 'Darling, what's wrong?'

Celia had to wait for the sobs to subside as she handed Kimberley a handkerchief to dab at her eyes. 'It's been three years Mum, three long years we've been trying for a baby with no success. We've had endless tests with the doctor and then with the hospital. We've even gone privately, Scott said if we had to pay we would. We've seen the best specialists in London and they all say there's nothing wrong with Scott or me, but it just isn't happening.'

'And now,' another surge of tears threatened to engulf Kimberley, 'Scott and I hardly ever see each other.'

'Surely, darling, you must stop Scott working so many hours. Tell him how you feel. I can see this is distressing you beyond measure.'

'But Mum, I can't, not at the moment. Scott is riding on the crest of a wave. He's waited for an opportunity like this to come up ever since he started at this company. It would be horribly selfish of me to spoil it for him now. He keeps saying that once this deal is completed and in the bag, we can get back to how it was when we were first married, when he had time for me.'

One thing Celia had given thanks for when Kimberley had first met Scott, was how attentive he was. Kimberley needed a man who would be demonstrative and caring, to make up for the fact that she always felt she had somehow failed her father. Anton, Celia's husband and Kimberley's father, was a good man but he had always wanted a boy and had longed for a son to carry on his doctor's practice as Anton had carried the family practice on from his father. But Kimberley, apart from being a girl, had been a slight child, skinny and prone to bouts of illness.

Anton used to see troops of patients through his private surgery who he labelled, 'the worried well,' and it had made him intolerant of weakness. 'I have to be the world's greatest actor,' he would boom out to Celia and Kimberley. 'Of all the people I saw today I would say that only two of them were really ill. The rest of them should go and do some work, get some exercise and stop stuffing their faces with expensive meals out, then they'd feel better. I deserve an Oscar for all the people I've sympathised with today about their petty worries.'

When Kimberley had been ill, she had stayed out of her father's way. She had also been aware of his lack of enthusiasm for all her small triumphs at school, such as prizes for art and lead parts in the school play. He always seemed much more interested in his friends' sons' efforts on the rugby pitch or their prowess at rowing. When his best friend, a surgeon in the local hospital, announced that his son was to row for Cambridge in the famous boat race, Kimberley saw Anton's face and knew that her efforts could never match up to her father's expectations. When she had had to confess to him that she had no intention of studying medicine and that law was her chosen field, she had seen the struggle he had made to wish her well.

Celia knew the crushing effect her father had had on Kimberley. So when Scott came along, Celia was delighted to see that not only was he an intelligent, strong, man, but he doted on her daughter and wasn't afraid to show it.

Kimberley had blossomed in his adoring love and in the first years of their marriage, she would delightedly phone Celia to tell her how Scott had bought flowers just because he wanted to; how he had taken time out of his day to seek out a particularly obscure classical CD she wanted; how he would tell her every night before going to sleep that he loved her.

But now Scott had another love in his life — his work. Celia felt despair run through her as she looked at her daughter's face, pale as a ghost's.

'Thanks, Mum, for being here and listening to me,' Kimberley said, and then looked momentarily puzzled. 'I meant to ask you, by the way, why on earth you and Cousin Grace were so distant? When you first talked about her I thought she must have been a bit of a hermit. I got the impression of some batty old woman living all on her own surrounded by millions of cats. But she wasn't like that at all. Everybody loved her. So why did she feel so cut off from us?'

'It was all very sad, really,' Celia said. 'As you know, Grace's father, your Uncle Sidney, was in the army, and in order not to disrupt Grace's education too much, they sent Grace to boarding school.'

'It was a terrible blow to her when Sidney and Mary had a second child, Simone, and, instead of sending her to boarding school, they kept Simone with them on their travels.'

'Why did they do that?'

'Well, Mary was a funny woman. When she had her first-born, I think she didn't know what had hit her, and a bout of post-natal depression meant she didn't bond with Grace as she should have. The other thing is, that Grace was rather a plain child, whereas Simone was gorgeous right from the beginning. She was very delicate, like a little doll, and smiled a lot. I think Mary just didn't like her first daughter as much as her second. Grace was always very mature and grown up about it, but I know it touched her deeply.'

'Anyway, Grace spent a lot of time with us when she was a teenager. She was a very bright girl, incredibly good at figures. She wanted to make something of herself; I think to prove to her parents that, although Simone was the one with the beauty, she was the one with the brains. While Simone was off being wooed by incredibly rich men — she married a South African diamond dealer and has more money than she knows what to do with — Grace buried her head in her studies. Because she was good with numbers she decided to become an accountant. She stayed with us while she studied and used to love going to classical concerts in London. That was where she met Tomasso.'

'Who's Tomasso?' Kimberley was intrigued.

'It's all rather sad, really. Tomasso was a young Italian, incredibly good looking. He was tall with wavy hair, and full of life. He was starting out in a promising career as a concert pianist and Grace met him when he played his debut at the Wigmore Hall. She was absolutely smitten with him. He was one of those men who drew people to him like a magnet. He was always surrounded by friends and she loved being in his company. What's more, he loved her. There was something about her cool Englishness which he seemed to find enchanting. After only a few weeks, he asked her to marry him.'

'But she didn't, did she? She still had our family name, Drake, until the day she died. What happened?'

'I'm afraid it was your father.'

'Dad?'

'Yes. But he did it out of the very best of intentions. You see, Grace was very young and so was Tomasso. We didn't know anything about him, we had no knowledge of his family and your father thought it was just a youthful infatuation on both their parts. Your father was also in a very difficult position. Sidney and Mary had been posted to Hong Kong, they were miles away and couldn't, or wouldn't, come home. Your father only asked Grace to wait, just asked her to give it time and not do anything silly like eloping, which I think she did have it in mind to do.'

'Your father pointed out that Tomasso was a young musician with not a penny to his name, while Grace came from a good family and, what's more, was heading towards a lucrative career.'

'When Tomasso asked her to marry him, he was just about to go off to do his first tour of America. He was booked to play Carnegie Hall and there was no way he could cancel. He asked Grace to go with him. He said that at the end of his tour, they could go to Hawaii and honeymoon there.'

'But your father kept up the pressure on Grace and made her stay here to continue her course and sit her exams. So instead of marrying and going to Hawaii on honeymoon with Grace, Tomasso was getting more and more lucrative offers to play in America. But he said he would come back to her, and I know they were very much in love. They spoke constantly on the phone and wrote to each other every day.'

'What happened when he came back?'

'He didn't.'

'What? He deserted her, after all?'

'No. He finally told her he simply couldn't live another moment without her and, despite getting further offers to play in the States, he booked on a plane to come back. But the plane crashed in Jamaica Bay, New York, killing everyone on board. They didn't even find his body. There was nothing for her to mourn, poor Grace. She even went out there, just to see where he'd died and I remember her telling us that one of the few comforts she had was that the area was so beautiful. There's a bird sanctuary nearby and Grace said that as Tomasso had such an eye for nature and beauty, that, at least, was some small thing she could hang on to. That was one of the last conversations I had with her.'

'Grace was absolutely distraught and although she qualified as an accountant, she kept herself to herself. Or rather, I should say she kept herself away from us. She blamed your father for persuading her to stay here and not go with Tomasso. She wrote to me once to say that if your father hadn't interfered, she and Tomasso would have been honeymooning in Hawaii and would have returned on a different plane at a different time and they would have married and had children. She loved children, absolutely loved them.'

'But Grace never found anyone else. I don't think there was anyone else for her. She'd lost her heart and she never found it again. She replaced what she had lost by concentrating on her career, but only because it gave her enough money to follow her real interests, which were The Sanctuary and the animals she cared for. I think she saw her animals as much more loving and loyal than human beings, who had failed her in so many ways.'

★ ★ ★

'Mum, do you think I've taken the wrong decision to keep The Sanctuary on?' They were pulling into Waterloo now and everyone was gathering bags and putting on coats.

Celia looked into her daughter's deep brown eyes and felt as worried as she had on Kimberley's first day at school, and as concerned as she had been when Kimberley had gone off to university.

She took her daughter's hand and held it tightly. 'I'm delighted you've got such a fantastic career and I think you've got a really wonderful marriage, but I know there's something missing for you at the moment. Maybe it's not quite so strange that Grace left you that house. Maybe, in some way, it will help you find what you need.'

As Celia kissed her daughter goodbye and headed for the Tube, she only hoped she was right. But Celia's heart was heavy. For, in reality, she had nearly reached out and stopped Kimberley's hand as she had signed the papers accepting the bequest of The Sanctuary. Only the enthusiastic smile on Kimberley's face had stopped her jumping in and shouting, 'No!'

Celia thought that taking on The Sanctuary was pure folly on her daughter's part and would only succeed in driving a wedge between her and Scott. But Celia's little girl was now an adult. The decision had been made. And that decision could cost Kimberley her marriage.

A Shock For Kimberley

As Kimberley waved goodbye to her mother, she decided to have a coffee at Waterloo before going back to the flat.

It had been a long, taxing day. Sitting at the coffee bar watching the world go by, a voice behind her cried, 'Hey, gorgeous, you come back to me after all this time.' With a broad grin on his face, the Italian waiter was still serving coffees. 'Latte wasn't it, pure pale coffee to match your beautiful complexion.'

'That's right, it is a latte, thank you.' Kimberley felt herself blush at the Italian's admiration and the fact that, amazingly, he had remembered her from this morning. Of course it was all show, he probably sold twice as many coffees to giggling office girls by doing his Romeo impression. But even if it was tosh, it gave a girl a lift.

Kimberley's father had rarely complimented her on her looks. He preferred the natural look to her polished city girl appearance and she had come to expect his negative comments about how much she spent on shampoo and make-up. It seemed like nothing she could do would win his approval. Whereas with Scott, it had always been different. He had made her feel like a princess. First thing in the morning, when Kimberley felt she looked her most ragged, she had often found Scott gazing at her as she read the morning paper and said he couldn't help it, she was too beautiful to ignore. Now, Kimberley reflected, she couldn't remember the last time they had sat relaxing over the morning papers.

'Maybe a croissant again, or we have an apricot Danish made with the finest Italian apricots,' the waiter said. It was almost too late for dinner now, so Kimberley gave in.

When the waiter arrived with the

steaming coffee and a delectable-looking Danish, he said, 'Enjoy. I think maybe you don't eat enough, you so slim. You look like a model, you should be on the catwalks of Milan.'

Kimberley just laughed and waved him away, as her mobile started bleeping.

It was Scott.

'Darling, it's been absolutely manic here. We've had meetings all through the day so it was difficult for me to get away. How are you?'

'I'm fine, thanks, tired but fine.'

'How's your mother, did you give her my love?'

'She's fine. She asked when we could go over for a meal with her and dad.'

'I don't know, things are a bit tight at the moment. Maybe when work calms down a bit.' There was a silence then as Kimberley hesitated. She should be telling Scott about her decision to take on The Sanctuary, but it didn't seem right to do it over the phone like this. Besides, she could hear people in the background, and she needed to talk to Scott alone, to get his undivided attention.

'Scott, where are you?' she asked.

'Still at work. The whole team's here, there's so much to do.' It was then that Kimberley noticed how strange Scott sounded. Maybe it was because he was over-tired. Then she heard a clatter of cups or glasses.

'Scott, are you in the pub or something?'

'No,' he laughed. 'No such luck. We've just had another pot of very strong coffee.' The noise of other people chatting got louder, so that Kimberley could hardly hear him. 'Hang on a minute, I'll close the door to my office, can't hear a thing with all this going on.' The sound of other people died as he shut the door. 'There, that's better. Sorry. Joe's been working us really hard today, I've never seen so much caffeine consumed in one day. I understand now how they keep going into the evening practically non-stop — the wheels are oiled by copious amounts of coffee.'

Scott was laughing, but Kimberley found it difficult to raise a smile. 'Anyway,' he went on, 'what happened today with the solicitor? Did he read you the will?'

'Yes, he read the will.'

'I guess you'll have to go and visit now and see what the old girl's place is like before you make a decision.'

'Actually,' Kimberley gulped, 'I've already seen it. We went today.'

'Crikey, that was quick. Couldn't you have waited until I could have gone with you?'

'When was that likely to be?'

The sound of voices drowned Scott out again. 'Look, I'm sorry, honey. We've just managed to get a conference call with America. We've been trying to get hold of them all day, so I'll have to go. Let's talk about your Cousin Grace's place when I get back later, huh?'

'Scott, it's already a quarter to ten. When are you coming home?'

'After this call. We'll just have one or two things to do after that, then I'll be home.' A strident male voice in the background, probably Joe Hatcher's thought Kimberley, shouted out, 'Come on, Scott, get in here or I'll find someone else to take the call.'

'Gotta go, love you,'

The line went dead and suddenly Kimberley didn't feel like eating her apricot Danish.

* * *

When she put her keys in the door of the flat, Kimberley felt exhausted. She had been subjected to such a mixture of emotions today. Taking off her coat and putting her briefcase under the hall table, she kicked off her shoes and made her way to the kitchen. As she stood waiting for the kettle to boil, to make herself a cup of tea while she waited for Scott to come home, she thought how very different life here was to life at The Sanctuary.

When she'd signed the papers that Mark Steyning had pushed towards her, she'd felt exhilarated. It was no exaggeration to say she'd fallen in love with The Sanctuary, perched on its little hill above the jewel blue cove. Everything about the place had seemed vibrant and real to her.

She looked around her kitchen now. It was as sparse and white and antiseptic as an operating theatre. The lines were clean and clinical, and she had loved that at first. It had seemed to say that she and Scott had made it. They were young professionals whose interests were work and other young professionals. Now that she thought about it, mused Kimberley, pouring boiling water on to a tea bag, every single person in their flats was under forty and worked in the city. They all went out in the day, worked long hours and only came back to sleep. Many of them had weekend homes. They didn't live here, these flats were like hotels. There was no balance here, no reality.

There were no old people, no middle-aged people and there most certainly weren't any children or pets. Kimberley smiled as she thought of Sigmund the donkey braying a welcome to any visitor to his home.

Kimberley's mind flitted to the young girl she had seen today. She was so lovely, and yet looking into her face was like looking at the surface of a calm sea. Yet Kimberley suspected that a depth of emotions was bubbling beneath the surface, and she felt a burning desire to help. Why wouldn't the girl talk? She had seemed troubled, and what was going on for her held more interest for Kimberley than all the e-mails she would shortly have to open which, when you got down to it, were only about companies making huge amounts of money for people who were already rich.

Taking her tea into the lounge, Kimberley stopped in her tracks. The place looked like a bomb had hit it. Or, at the very least, that a large amount of drinking and eating had taken place.

There was an empty bottle of champagne, two glasses, one of which had been knocked over and lay in pieces on the normally pristine coffee table, and crumbs from peanuts and packets of crisps had been trodden into the carpet.

So, she thought bitterly, Scott had been too busy to call her all day, working on his important business deals. But he hadn't been too busy to come back here with someone and have an impromptu liquid lunch. What's more, she had left the flat looking beautiful this morning, and now it was in this state, presumably for her to clear up. The final straw was a saucer full of cigarette butts. Scott had mentioned that Joe Hatcher smoked, so Kimberley guessed he had been the guest who had been entertained here today.

Putting down her tea, her blood boiling, Kimberley went to the kitchen for the dustpan and brush and cleared up the broken glass. She threw away the empty champagne bottle and the saucer with the cigarette butts.

The place only looked restored to order after she had polished the coffee table and Hoovered the carpet. Taking her now cold tea with her, Kimberley went to check her e-mails, all the while fuming.

It was midnight before she finally conceded that Scott wasn't going to be back until the early hours of the morning, and she finally fell into bed. The last thing she did was to send him a text saying she wasn't going to wait up any longer. As she pressed the button and it lit up into life, she saw that there was a text to her from him.

'Sorry darling, still at work. Don't wait up. Love you more than ever. Scott xxx.'

Well, she supposed, at least he'd managed that much communication today. She rolled over feeling cold and lonely before slipping into an uneasy sleep.

Scott Visits The Sanctuary

'You don't seriously mean to tell me that you said 'yes' to taking on that scuzzy old house?' Scott said.

'It is not scuzzy, whatever that means.'

'It means, that in a moment of madness, you've taken on a complete and utter white elephant and what's more there's probably a herd of white elephants in the back garden from what you've told me. Donkeys, rabbits, swans, it's madness, Kimberley! How in Heaven's name are we meant to look after that lot when we're so far away? They'll starve or catch something. We'll have the RSPCA down on us. It simply isn't practical.'

'Scott, I told you, there's a really nice woman, Florence Wise and her two daughters who used to help Cousin Grace and now they're helping us. I'm keeping Florence on and giving her a bit of a raise in salary because she'll be doing most of the work on her own now.'

'And how are we meant to afford that?'

'Oh, come on Scott, it's not much, and we've got more than enough.'

'And I suppose that pile of old bricks needs repairing and re-decorating. That'll cost us a fortune.'

'Mostly it just needs a lick of paint and cleaning and I'm happy to do that. In fact, I think I might enjoy doing something practical at the weekends. It'll make a change from sitting at the computer all day.'

'I just wish you'd consulted me before you signed on the dotted line.'

'And I just wish you'd come and see The Sanctuary before judging it.'

A heavy silence hung in the air and an even heavier feeling settled in Kimberley's heart. 'Anyway, I would have consulted you if I'd been able to get hold of you. You're never there to speak to, Scott, and when you are, I'm not sure you're even listening to me.'

Kimberley walked over to the balcony's sliding glass doors and opened them for a breath of fresh air. What met her was the wailing of sirens from the street below. Sometimes, the city just wore her out, she reflected, as she closed the door and thought back to the calling of the gulls and peaceful lull of the sea at The Sanctuary.

'I'm not sure I can fit in a visit down there at the moment. It's not exactly up the road, is it?' Scott said.

'Please Scott, it's not that far. Anyway, they're not making you work at weekends now, are they?'

'Actually, I've got a pile of files to read before Monday. I'll have to do them at the weekend.'

'You could bring them down with you.'

He sighed, and she could sense him weakening.

* * *

They'd started off this conversation with a blazing row about the state Scott and Joe Hatcher had left the flat in. Scott had always taken as much pride in their surroundings as Kimberley had. And besides, one of the reasons she loved Scott was because he was fair in everything. He wasn't one of those chauvinist males who go around thinking the rest of the world is there to clear up after them.

They were both exhausted with this argument, standing, arms crossed, glaring at each other. Now, Scott let out a sigh, dropped his arms and came towards her in a gesture of peace. As he opened his arms, she fell into them, folding herself around him. He stroked her hair, the way he always used to. 'Why does this place mean so much to you?'

'I don't know, Scott, I really don't know.'

'Okay, I give in. If it really is that important to you, let's go down there together this weekend and you can show it to me.'

'Oh Scott, thank you. I really want you to see it. I think it'll do you good to get away, too. I know the Tavistock deal means everything to you, but there are other things in life.'

'Of course there are.' He kissed the top of her head in that tender way she was so familiar with and said, 'I'm sorry I left the flat in such a state. It was thoughtless of me. Joe's such a charismatic character, he sort of sweeps everything and everyone along with him. I guess that's why he's so successful. I wish I was like him.'

'Oh, no, Scott, I love you just the way you are. Don't change. Especially not into Joe Hatcher.'

★   ★   ★

It didn't feel so much like February, more like April, as they drove down in the BMW, the newly-ploughed fields of Hampshire laid out like sheets of brown paper. Kimberley felt happy and secure. They both needed this break; it would be good for them. Already, despite the fact that he had packed a briefcase full of documents to read, Kimberley could feel some of the stress Scott had been under the past weeks melting away.

In his sunglasses, white, long-sleeved T-shirt and jeans, he looked no older than the first day she had met him at uni. They'd had so many dreams then; about passing their exams, being successful in their careers, living the good life, and so much of it had come true. And, as they'd fallen in love and planned to marry, they'd talked about children. Scott would make such a wonderful father. He'd loved sport at uni and had talked a lot early on about how he could explain the offside rule and the techniques of overarm bowling to a son. But then, gradually, as their efforts had led to nothing, Scott had stopped talking about children.

Kimberley wondered how much he thought about them now. The subject had almost become taboo. Normally, any time Kimberley's thoughts turned to the baby she couldn't have, she felt utterly miserable. But today, somehow the sunshine, the thought of going to stay by the sea and making plans for doing up The Sanctuary had pushed the pain away.

'You know, I've been thinking,' Scott said.

'About what?' asked Kimberley.

'About this car.'

'What about it?'

'I think we should get a new one.'

'Why? There's nothing wrong with the BMW and we haven't had it that long.'

'It's just that Joe laughed when he saw it.'

'What?'

'He reckoned it was a bit downmarket, a bit of a chav's car, was how he put it.'

'What rubbish, Scott. It gets us from A to B and it's comfortable.'

'Yeah, I guess so, but maybe it's about time to go for a newer model.'

'Well, if you must, but it's never

worried you before.'

'Maybe I'll just look around, have a think about it. We might need two cars, anyway, if you're going to be going down to The Sanctuary every weekend.'

'I suppose so,' Kimberley reluctantly agreed, 'but really, we hardly ever use the car in London. It mainly sits in the garage unless you're late for work and I have to get you there in double quick time. It seems a bit of an extravagance to have two.'

'Maybe.' Scott didn't sound convinced and Kimberley decided that if a second car would make him happy, then it wasn't worth making a fuss about.

'I've never met Joe, or his wife,' she said, trying to get the subject off cars.

Scott laughed. 'You're not likely to meet his wife. He doesn't have one. At the moment, that is.'

'What do you mean, at the moment?'

'Well, to be honest, he's not that good at holding on to them. He's been divorced three times.'

'Three times? That's ridiculous.'

'I know, that's what he says. He now says he's not going to bother to get married again, but he doesn't seem short of girlfriends.'

'How old is he?'

'I don't know exactly, late forties I suppose.'

'That's a bit old to be having a string of girlfriends, isn't it? Maybe he should grow up a bit.'

'Become a responsible married man, like me, you mean?' Scott smiled.

'Yes,' Kimberley squeezed his arm playfully. 'Like you.'

★ ★ ★

The sea crossing was as calm as the first time. 'It's a pretty island, isn't it?' said Scott, as they drove down country lanes and passed gardens full of tulips.

'Wait until you see Highview Cove.'

When they got to the car park at the top of the cliff, Kimberley was as excited as a schoolgirl as they unloaded their bags and made their way down the narrow path. As they got to the bottom and the cove opened out in front of them, Scott gasped. 'Wow,' he said, 'I can see why it made such an impression on you.' The sea lay before them with the morning sun twinkling on it like a thousand diamonds.

'And that,' Kimberley said, like she was unveiling a prize sculpture, 'is The Sanctuary.'

'Hmm, interesting.'

As they walked up to the gate, there was the familiar braying as Sigmund came lolloping down to meet them. 'Hello boy,' Scott said as he stroked him. 'Is this the guard dog?' he asked Kimberley.

'Sort of. Come and see the house.'

★ ★ ★

Kimberley unlocked the door and gave Scott the grand tour.

'So, what do you think?' she asked breathlessly as they had finished looking at the lounge, the kitchen, the animals outside, and had ended up in the master bedroom, which was bathed in warm sunlight. Her heart dropped as she saw that Scott's face had a look of distaste on it.

'I don't suppose it's had a carpenter or a builder anywhere near it in years. And although your cousin might have been a whiz with animals, I don't reckon she'd ever been in a do-it-yourself shop. These walls look as if they've got the paint on from the year the house was built.' Kimberley could feel her muscles tensing as she sensed what was coming. 'And these curtains, which I suppose must have once been white, are just horribly yellow now.'

'Okay,' said Kimberley, her voice flat, 'so you don't like it. I somehow knew you wouldn't, but I did so hope . . . '

Scott grabbed her hands. 'I love it!'

'What?'

'I'm just winding you up.'

Kimberley jumped up and down like an excited puppy and playfully whacked Scott on the arm before hugging him.

'That's not to say,' he said, 'that it doesn't need a heck of a lot of work doing on it, because it does. You must be completely mad to have taken it on, but I think, in your position, I would have done the same thing myself. It's a beautiful old house, full of character and with the most amazing view.'

★ ★ ★

They went downstairs and made toasted currant buns. They had just finished eating when they heard a knock at the door. 'Florence!' cried Kimberly, 'I'm so pleased to see you. I need to know what to do with our current animal guests. I see the swans have gone.'

'That's right,' said Florence, coming in with a box full of fruit, vegetables and pet food. 'They've gone off to a sanctuary on the mainland, but we're expecting a new patient any minute now.'

'Here, let me take that,' Scott said.

'This must be your husband.'

'That's right.' Scott deposited the box on the dining table and shook Florence's hand, receiving a hearty shake in return. 'Very pleased I am to meet you. I cleared out all the pens yesterday and there's three plastic bags of rubbish to go up to the car park.'

'I've got to get another bag from the car,' Scott said, 'I'll take them up now if you show me where they are.'

Once Scott was on his way, Florence came back, beaming all over her face as she said to Kimberley, 'What a lovely man your husband is. My Mike was the best man ever, but you could never call him no oil painting. Your Scott, though, well, he looks like one of them men you see in posh magazines selling aftershave and the like, doesn't he? Nice to have something good to look at over the breakfast table, that's what I say! Anyway, if you'll help me Kimberley, we need to get some bedding and a few other things out of the shed for our new arrival.'

Kimberley followed Florence into a large, beautifully organised shed at the back of the garden. On its shelves were rows of pet dishes, squeaky toys, small plastic baths, cushions, blankets and everything needed for every kind of animal.

'If you could take that,' Florence handed Kimberley a large, clean, padded dog bed and a gaily coloured blanket, 'and I'll bring these,' she said, taking shampoo, a brush, nail clippers and a dog collar from the shelf. 'I had a call last night from a vet in Sandown. He's had a golden retriever brought in to him in a bit of a state. Poor thing was found wandering in the road, matted, covered in fleas and starving hungry. He had a collar on with a tag so the police went to see his owner. The man who owns him is one of those aimless people who can barely look after himself, poor soul, let alone an animal. He admitted he hadn't enough money to pay for dog food and was only giving him dusting powder bought in the shops to clear the fleas, but the infestation had got too bad. He gave the dog up willingly to the authorities.'

Kimberley followed Florence into the utility room at the back of the house. Set up as a little treatment room, it had a large, scrubbed, white counter, a double sink and cupboards full of medication and implements. Towels, neatly folded, sat on shelves above the sink. When a knock came at the front door, Scott, who had arrived back, went to answer it.

The policeman didn't stay long as he had to rush off to attend to another call, but he left with them a scrawny, but lively-looking, dog.

'There we are,' said Florence, 'let's have you out to the back and get you all clean.'

'What breed is he?' asked Scott. 'I'd say he was a golden retriever, he's got those lovely soulful eyes, but he doesn't look big enough.'

Florence lifted the dog up on to the table in the treatment room and stroked his head. His tail started to wag as soon as he realised he was among friends. 'He is a retriever, it's just that he's so skinny and his coat's so matted, you'd hardly recognise the breed.'

Florence took a tape measure out of the drawer and carefully wound it around the dog at its thinnest point.

'There, look at that, he should be nearly twice that size.'

'Now, we log the animal's measurements and weight down in this daybook with the day they arrived, so we can monitor their progress.'

'If you was to go in the lounge later, Kimberley, when you have more time, and look up Miss Grace's journals, you'll be able to find every reference way back over the years when we've had retrievers in here. She used to put down everything.'

'This boy'll do fine once he's had a few decent meals inside him, but first of all we need to get rid of these fleas.'

'Fleas!' Scott and Kimberley cried in unison.

'Don't worry,' laughed Florence, 'they'll all be dead now. The vet has some pretty strong stuff. But he needs a thorough shampoo now. The vet told me he'd given him some antibiotics to clear that bit of skin infection he's got there. See, poor thing's been scratching and it's set up those nasty sore patches.'

'Perhaps after I've shampooed him, you'd give what's left of his coat a gentle brush, Kimberley? He'd like that.'

'Yes, of course. What's his name?'

'His owner called him Ben.'

'Ben it is,' said Kimberley, smiling as the dog turned his head and wagged his tail

That evening, Ben sat, smelling like roses, at Kimberley's feet, as she started to read through Cousin Grace's journals. He was keener on sitting by her than sitting in his bed, and it was comforting to feel his warmth against her as she sat in the armchair. Every now and then, she'd reach down and

143

stroke him. As soon as Florence had finished his bath, they had fed him, and he'd wolfed down the food as if it was his first meal for days. Which it probably was, Florence thought sadly. Now, all cleaned up and brushed, he really was the prettiest of dogs, with large, soulful eyes.

'He likes you,' said Scott.

'I think he just likes women. And he looks better already, don't you think?'

'Yes,' said Scott, looking up from the work papers he had brought with him, 'and so do you, Kimberley.' She smiled at him, perfectly content, and wishing every evening could be like this.

* * *

The next morning, Kimberley found that she woke earlier than normal. She decided to leave Scott to catch up on his rest. Dawn was just glimmering over the horizon as, showered and dressed in a thick green polo neck, she opened the lounge windows, breathed in the crisp sea air and looked out towards the beach.

It was a long time since she had seen anything so wondrously beautiful. The sky was like a block of strawberry and raspberry ice-cream. The aquamarine of night was giving way to heliotrope tipped with shell pink and tangerine. As she watched the colours shimmer, a broad yellow sun appeared on the horizon and started to rise. It only lasted five minutes, after which all the reds and oranges drifted away, leaving a clear yellow sun which glistened on the shore. The tide was low and as Ben had come to sit beside her, wagging his tail expectantly, Kimberley said, 'I guess it's time for your walk, isn't it?'

She put a lead on him, which proved difficult, as he seemed more intent on licking her hand.

They set out down the path, through the gate, over the concrete sea path and on to the beach, which was deserted. Ben seemed slightly nervous to be out in the open and Kimberley guessed that he had been kept inside a lot. He stuck to her like glue, walking so close, she almost tumbled over him. It would be good, though, for him to run around a bit, and Kimberley decided to take a chance and let him off the lead. The cove was quite safe — at one end the path simply petered out into the sea, so it was really like a dead end with the only exit being the path that led off up to the cliffs. She would keep a close eye on him and if he looked as if he was straying in that direction, she could catch him and put the lead back on again.

But Ben showed no signs of wanting to escape. He snuffled around happily, taking a few steps into the water, getting his belly wet and then running back to Kimberley.

Kimberley was concentrating so hard on Ben, she almost didn't see the young girl hunkered down, peering into a rock pool and turning something over with a small stick.

Kimberley stopped in her tracks. It

146

was the teenager with the blonde hair she had seen the day she came here with Mark Steyning and Celia. Today, the girl was wearing denim shorts, canvas yachting shoes and a thick, red, hooded top. The hood was up and she was almost buried in it, as if she didn't want anybody to invade her space. Kimberley was about to turn away and leave her in peace, but Ben had other ideas and set off at a trot to investigate. With the hood hiding her face, the girl hadn't noticed him until he shook himself from head to tail, releasing a shower of water which splashed over her legs. She gasped, stood up, then, when she realised it was a dog that had splashed her, reached out and hugged him to her.

'Hello,' said Kimberley, at which the girl jumped and retreated backwards. For a moment Kimberley thought the girl would run away again. But her beautiful hazel eyes had settled on Ben, and she hunkered down and reached her hand out towards him. The girl's hood had fallen off and her long wavy blonde hair lifted gently in the breeze as she crouched motionless with a worried look in her eyes.

'He won't bite you, he's as soft as butter,' Kimberley said.

The girl ran her hand gingerly over Ben's sparse coat. She looked up at Kimberley and her eyes seemed to be full of questions, but she said nothing. She was examining Ben and at one point let her hand gently rest on one of his bald patches.

Kimberley's words of explanation came tumbling out. 'He's a rescue dog, we're looking after him because he's been left to get in that state and we're trying to make him better. The vet's given him some medicine and the salt water won't do him any harm. Sometimes it can be quite healing. He's a happy dog, just a bit timid and much too skinny.'

The girl's eyes were full of compassion and, as Ben came closer, she cradled his face in her hands, smiling when he licked her. Then she wrapped the dog in her arms and hugged him, nuzzling her head into his neck.

'What's your name?' asked Kimberley, when the girl had stopped hugging Ben, who had gone off to sniff at a stone.

The girl hesitated, unsmiling, her hazel eyes hooded. Then, looking at Ben again, she seemed to relent and opened her mouth. But nothing came out. She closed it and opened it again, then in a gesture of pure frustration, hit her fist into the sand. Feeling helpless, Kimberley wanted to tell the girl not to be frightened, that she didn't mean any harm, and then it occurred to her that, for some reason, the girl couldn't talk.

Kimberley had a shot of inspiration. Picking up the stick the girl had been holding, she started to write in the sand, K-I-M-B-E-R-L-E-Y. 'Kimberley, that's my name. What's yours?'

The girl inclined her head to one side, took the stick and wrote L-A-U-R-E-N. 'Lauren, that's a lovely name.

Pleased to meet you, Lauren.' Kimberley held out her hand but the girl didn't take it.

'What were you looking at in the rock pool?' Kimberley changed the subject, anxious not to intimidate the girl. Ben was, at this moment, looking into the pool with his ears up and gingerly tapping at something with his paw.

The girl smiled, stroking Ben as she gently pulled him away and kept him close to her. When Kimberley looked in the rock pool she saw a blue lobster moving around in the shallow water, his antennae waving.

The girl grabbed the stick again and wrote in the sand, 'Too young, must go back in the water.'

'Of course. Do the young ones get caught in the rock pools often?'

The girl rapidly nodded her head.

'And you save them?'

Lauren smiled and nodded. Then, releasing Ben, she bent down into the pool, dipped the stick in front of the lobster until he grabbed it with his large claws, then deftly reached in, grasped him by the back of the shell and, holding him at arms' length, ran down to the water's edge where she let him scuttle back into the sea. Ben, who was intent on playing with this new toy, leapt into the waves until the girl showed him the stick and threw it on the sand for him. Luckily, Ben decided Lauren was more fun to play with than the lobster and ran joyfully after the stick, picking it up and depositing it back at her feet. For the first time since Kimberley had seen her, Lauren looked like a carefree, normal girl. Her hair blew in the breeze as she turned round and round, laughing, with Ben jumping up to grasp the stick.

* * *

Kimberley sat on a rock near the front gardens of the cottages which faced the sea as she watched Ben and Lauren playing when, unexpectedly, a deep voice behind her asked, 'Would you like a coffee?' Startled, she turned to see a tall man standing in his shingle garden with a full cafetiere in one hand and two mugs in the other. He put them down on his low wall made from sea rocks and poured two steaming mugs of coffee, handing one to Kimberley. She wrapped her hands around the hot mug and took a gulp. 'Thank you.'

'Well, you've earned it,' said the man, whose dark eyes looked at her intently underneath a fringe of wayward black curls.

'I have?' Kimberley said.

'Yes. Anyone who can make my daughter forget her troubles, even for five minutes, has earned far more than a cup of coffee.'

So this was the man who Florence thought looked like a gypsy and, according to her, never smiled. He did look preoccupied, mused Kimberley, but certainly not as fierce as Florence had claimed.

'She's a lovely girl, although she doesn't say much,' Kimberley ventured.

'Well, thank you for being so polite, when what you really meant to say, was that my daughter simply doesn't speak.'

'I suppose maybe I was being a bit too tactful. But I didn't want to offend you, or your daughter, in any way.'

'I don't mind holding my hand up and declaring that to other people, Lauren must seem decidedly odd. Poor little mite, she wasn't always like that. She does have a voice, hearing her laughing was what brought me outside just now. It's too long a time since I heard that. To say you've made my day would be the understatement of the century.'

'So if she isn't incapable of speaking, if she does, as you say, have a voice, why doesn't she speak?'

'It's a long story,' the man said, and Kimberley saw the emotional shutters come down. 'Watch out, she's coming this way with that scrawny dog of yours, and if she knows we're talking about her she'll cut off from you altogether, and I'd really rather she didn't. Lauren needs all the friends she can get. Look,' the man said quickly in a whisper, 'what's your name?'

'Kimberley.'

'Did I see you walking from the big house, from The Sanctuary?'

'Yes, that's right. I'll be down regularly at weekends, I've just taken it over.'

'Good, please come back and see us — see Lauren — again, won't you? Please.' His deep chocolate brown eyes were earnest with pleading. 'You've just achieved what an army of doctors, speech therapists and counsellors haven't been able to manage in the last three months.'

At the sound of Lauren's feet crunching on the pebbly path, he suddenly assumed a lighter air and said, 'my name's Zach, Zachary Coen, but Zach to my friends. It's really nice to meet you, Kimberley. I look forward to seeing you again.'

Lauren's expression was questioning, even suspicious, as she approached them, holding on to Ben's collar so the dog couldn't run away. Kimberley tried to keep her voice matter of fact and, jumping off the wall where she'd been sitting, she said, 'I'd be happy to see you any time up at the house, Lauren. Come and see Sigmund. Just open the gate and let yourself in. He loves having visitors.'

Lauren managed a shy smile and Zach said, 'That's very kind of you. Lauren was worried the other day that you'd think she was trespassing, coming in to see the donkey like that.'

'No, of course not,' answered Kimberley. 'And I'll let Florence, the lady who looks after the sanctuary when we're not there, know you're to be allowed in at any time. Sigmund loves carrots, by the way, and potato and apple peelings.'

Not wanting to scare Lauren off by being overly familiar, Kimberley sensed it was time for her to go. She was touched to see how Lauren gave Ben one last cuddle as she kissed his scraggy head fondly. She was sure she saw Lauren whispering into Ben's ear before the dog bounded back to her. So Lauren could talk, even if it was only to animals.

★ ★ ★

'Who was that I saw you talking to?' Scott was drying his hair by the French windows as Kimberley went into the bedroom. The room was warm with the sunlight streaming into it, and Kimberley could see that, from up here, Scott had a grandstand view of the whole of the bay.

'His name's Zachary Coen and he has a daughter, Lauren, who I met the other day.'

'And a wife?'

'Not that I've seen. Florence says the girl doesn't have a mother, so maybe not.'

'And he spends his time chatting up beautiful women.'

'He wasn't chatting me up,' laughed Kimberley.

'So the fact that he's tall, fit and looks like a rock star completely passed you by?'

'Well, yes, actually,' Kimberley said, going over and kissing Scott. 'Why would I look twice at anyone else when I've got the most gorgeous man in the whole world standing before me looking delectable?'

'Hmm,' replied Scott, 'flattery will get you anywhere. What's for breakfast?'

An Unfulfilled Longing

Kimberley had sat in this surgery so many times before and every time, she hoped the news would be good. 'Well,' said Dr Carstairs, taking off his glasses and putting down the notes in front of him, 'there really is no reason at all that I can see from these tests that you can't have a baby, and I told Scott the same thing the other day when he came for his appointment. It's a shame the two of you couldn't have come here together, but I believe he's incredibly busy at work at the moment.'

'Yes.' Kimberley's tone was flat.

'You know, Nature decrees in its own wonderful way that humans, like any other creature, are more likely to have babies if they're relaxed. You both need to slow down and take it easy. Can't you get away for a bit?'

'We spent this weekend by the sea

and it was absolute bliss.'

'Then my prescription for you two is more of the same, as often as possible.'

'But I'm not getting any younger, Doctor,' Kimberley protested.

'You're not old, Kimberley, not by a long shot. You have time on your side. Believe me.'

★　★　★

Kimberley walked through one of the leafy London squares, not wanting to go back yet to the loneliness of an empty flat. She sat down on a bench and watched the people going by. At the end of the square was a small playground with swings and slides and funny wonky animals on springs that children could sit on.

Most of the office workers had gone to work, and the square was now filled with older retired people, students, and mothers with small children. A mother with a pram strolled by Kimberley. Inside the pram was a tiny bundle wrapped in a white jumpsuit with rabbit ears. Kimberley could just see the baby's doll-like head and its scrunched up little eyes as it slept. Beside the mother was a little girl around three years old with the most perfect blonde baby curls, so delicate they seemed to drift in the breeze as the little child ran with excitement to get on one of the bouncy animals. As the mother passed by Kimberley, she chanced to look at her and smile and it was a smile of such perfect pleasure and serenity, Kimberley felt it wrench at her heart.

At one time she would have said something to the mother, complimented her on having such a beautiful child and gone over to marvel at what a good-tempered baby she had. But now she found she could only just force a smile and turn quickly away. The unmet need within her was so great, she was beginning to have difficulty finding comfort in the joy of others, and she hated herself for it. Resolutely, she got up and started walking the other way. It would take her twice as long to get back home, but today, she simply couldn't walk through the children's playground and see the watchful mothers. The hope it had given her in the past, thinking that she would one day be one of them, had all but disappeared.

★ ★ ★

Kimberley hardly saw Scott the rest of the week. He had to go away in connection with the Tavistock deal to Manchester, then to Sheffield, Birmingham and Carlisle.

The few times she had managed to speak to him, he was breathless with excitement, having met all the top people in his company's offices around the country. 'How on earth are you keeping going?' Kimberley had said worriedly to him on one of their all too infrequent phone calls.

'Well, it is tough. We have meetings from first thing to last thing at night, but Joe's assured me it won't be like this forever. And he has his various tactics to keep himself going.'

'Like what?' Kimberley frowned.

'Mainly whisky and endless cups of coffee so strong you could stand a spoon up in them,' Scott laughed.

'Scott, I don't think that sort of lifestyle does anyone any good. Are you eating properly and getting enough sleep?'

'Joe doesn't seem to need much sleep, and it's amazing how much you can do without when you need to.'

Kimberley had gone sadly into the kitchen after that conversation and looked at all the fresh green spinach and lettuce and the bright orange peppers and butternut squash she was going to prepare for her lunch, wondering what Scott would have that day. He used to be so careful of his health.

At the end of the week, though, Scott had agreed to go back to the Isle of Wight with her. He'd popped in that

Friday afternoon to deposit his over-night bag, but said he would have to go back to the office again and that Kimberley should pick him up in the BMW at 7 p.m. to leave for The Sanctuary.

Kimberley opened the bag. 'I don't see you all week and this is what you bring me back, a pile of dirty washing.'

'Sorry, darling.' Scott kissed her, then quickly grabbed some files.

'Scott, this shirt absolutely stinks of smoke. You haven't taken up smoking, have you?'

'No, I haven't, although loads of the guys do. We had a meeting at Joe's flat the other day and the air was thick with it. He said he used to smoke a lot more, but he's had to cut down lately, what with the smoking ban.'

As he was shrugging back into his jacket, Scott delved in the pocket and said, 'I didn't just get you a load of dirty washing while I was away. I got you this as well.'

'I saw it in a jeweller's in Sheffield

and it reminded me of you.'

Surprised and pleased by the unexpected gift, Kimberley opened the box Scott gave her and there inside, nestling on a bed of blue velvet, was a gold charm bracelet. On it were a collection of animal charms, a donkey, a little goat, a dog who looked just like Ben and a swan. It was perfect, and so touching.

'I think about you all the time when I'm away,' Scott said softly, and kissed her. 'Gotta go, darling. See you at seven. Love you.'

'Love you too.' But before she'd finished the words, Scott was out the door.

Kimberley Gets To Know Lauren

Scott fell asleep as soon as they hit the motorway, and barely woke up until they got to The Sanctuary. Once there, he was asleep as soon as his head hit the pillow. He must be exhausted, thought Kimberley, as she sat having her coffee on the balcony the next morning.

It worried her how hard he was working, with hardly any sleep, during the week. No wonder at the weekend he just flaked out. He was still fast asleep, now, even though the daylight was streaming into the bedroom. The weather had changed over the past week, the endless unseasonal sunshine giving way to brisk, chilly winds. But Kimberley still liked to sit outside and watch the waves crashing onto the sand. She was well wrapped up in corduroy trousers, a thick cable knit jumper and a woollen jacket with a hood.

Ben was sitting beside her, his head facing into the wind, seeming to enjoy the wildness of the breeze in the way that dogs do.

Once they had brought their bags down last night and unlocked the house, the first thing Kimberley had done was to fetch Ben from Florence's.

'There, what d'you think of him?' Florence had said.

Ben went over, eager for a stroke. 'He's looking fantastic, Florence! You're doing a wonderful job. His coat's beginning to grow back and it's lost a lot of that roughness. He feels really soft now, the way a retriever should. And those ribs are beginning to disappear. I take it he's eating well?'

'Oh dear me, yes. He's such a happy dog, he just needs a bit of tender loving care, that's all.'

'What are we going to do with him long term, though? I was reading Cousin Grace's journals last night and she said the most difficult thing with all the animals is letting them go, because you can easily get attached to all of them and end up running a zoo rather than a sanctuary.'

'Well, that's right m'dear. He is a super dog, but you just can't keep 'em all. Finding a good home for Ben is going to be one of your first challenges.'

Kimberley looked down at Ben now in the early morning light and stroked his head. It wouldn't be fair to keep him. Florence was great, but she had pets of her own and didn't need another one and as she and Scott were only here at weekends, they couldn't leave him at The Sanctuary. It would be unfair to keep him in the flat. Retrievers were big dogs who needed lots of exercise and the chance to run around. London wasn't suited to that. And in any case, Kimberley and Scott would never find time during the week to look after Ben properly.

★ ★ ★

As she looked down over the cove, Kimberley heard Sigmund bray, and then into view came Lauren, clutching a plastic bag. Kimberley was pleased to see that she had taken her at her word and was letting herself in through the gate. It looked as if giving Sigmund his breakfast had become part of her morning routine.

'Come on Ben, let's go down and say hello.'

Ben bounded over to Lauren and a smile instantly lit up her previously serious face. He jumped up and she laughed as he licked her and went round and round her in circles. 'He's pleased to see you,' Kimberley said.

Lauren nodded enthusiastically, as if to say that the feeling was mutual.

While she finished giving Sigmund the last of his feed, Ben stood at Lauren's feet, looking up expectantly. She looked down at him with her expressive eyes and shook the bag upside down as if to say she was sorry there was nothing in there for him.

'I don't think it's food he's after, he's just had a huge bowlful. It's his early morning walk he wants,' Kimberley said. At that, Ben took up his lead in his mouth and stood looking imploringly first at Kimberley, then at Lauren. And at that moment, Kimberley had an idea.

'Lauren, could you do me a huge favour? Ben desperately needs a walk, but I've got the animals to feed and I also had a phone call last night saying that an injured fox is being brought in. Do you think you could take Ben for a walk along the beach?'

Lauren's eyes lit up with joy and she held her hands in front of her and enfolded them to her chest, almost as if she was praying. Then, in a gesture which was so unexpected it nearly knocked Kimberley over, Lauren came over to her and enfolded her in a hug. 'I'll take that as a yes, then,' laughed Kimberley.

Lauren nodded happily.

'Okay,' Kimberley said, 'but you must

keep him on the lead at first so he knows it's you he should be sticking with. But then, if you think it's safe enough, you could let him off for a bit, but still keep a very close eye on him. Can you do that?'

Lauren nodded, and picked up Ben's lead. 'Do you have a watch?' Lauren rolled up the sleeve of her grey hoodie and showed Kimberley her watch. 'Good. I think about a twenty-minute walk should be fine, although if he hasn't exhausted you by then, you can keep him for half an hour maximum.' Lauren smiled enthusiastically and patted Ben. 'Okay then, have fun.'

Kimberley opened the gate and watched the two of them break into a run, Ben barking and all the time looking up at Lauren as they ran.

★ ★ ★

Half an hour wasn't so long, but while Kimberley was feeding the animals at the back, she couldn't help constantly popping back to the lounge to have a look at the cove from the balcony to see how Lauren was getting on. Kimberley deliberately stood to the side so Lauren couldn't see she was checking up on her but actually, Lauren was doing a great job. For the first twenty minutes, she kept Ben on a lead, and the two of them ran up and down the beach, chasing the crashing waves. Then, tentatively, Lauren let Ben off the lead, but Kimberley was touched to see how she sat the dog down and whispered instructions in his ear before letting him go. Ben seemed as smitten with Lauren as she was with him, and the only time he left her side was when she threw a stick for him.

When Kimberley looked at her watch and saw that the half hour was almost up, she was gratified to hear Sigmund announcing Lauren and Ben's return, and answered the knock at the door giving every impression that she had forgotten the time, rather than that she had been surreptitiously watching them.

'Well, he looks better for that. Do you want to come in and help dry him off?' she said.

Lauren looked hesitant and, when Kimberley gave her a puzzled look, Lauren pointed outside to her cottage. 'Ah, you want to tell your father where you are?'

Lauren nodded.

'That's fine. Tell you what, come in and give him a ring, the phone's over there and while you're doing that, I'll make us both a nice cup of hot chocolate. My hands are freezing after feeding the . . . ' Kimberley stopped, noticing that Lauren was standing with her dark hazel eyes looking down, her fists balled at her side.

'Oh, Lauren, I'm so sorry, I wasn't thinking. Of course you can't phone him. How silly of me. But I can give him a ring, can't I? Here, write his number on this pad and I'll call him right now.'

Lauren put her hand out to settle on Kimberley's arm in a gesture of thanks, and Kimberley was sure she saw the girl's eyes brim with tears.

'Here,' she said quickly, 'take this towel and give Ben a rub down out the back. He's covered in sand.'

* * *

When Kimberley reached Zach on the phone, he was elated. 'I wondered where she'd got to, but when I saw her out there with your dog, I was delighted. Do you know, I haven't seen her looking so happy or confident in a long time.'

'I offered to get her a pet a while ago, thinking it might help to bring her out of herself, but she hasn't shown any spark of enthusiasm until now.'

'I suppose it's because Ben needs someone so desperately,' Kimberley said. 'He's a bit damaged emotionally, poor thing, and maybe Lauren sees in him a creature who needs help and that resonates with her.'

'I guess so,' said Zach thoughtfully. 'But what on earth can I do to thank you?'

'Oh, don't worry, it was nothing. But if I can keep Lauren for a while, she can help me a bit around here. I've got tons of things to do and I just don't know where to start.'

'Do you think she'd be any good at clearing out a few pens?'

'Absolutely. If she wants to, then go for it.'

'Great. We're expecting an injured fox in later today and she can help me get things ready for it.'

So it was settled, and Lauren was so keen to help that, once Kimberley had shown her what to do, she intimated that she wanted to do the work all on her own, leaving Kimberley free to take down the curtains that so desperately needed washing.

Kimberley filled the whole of the long washing line that ran from the house down the hill with flapping, now clean, curtains, so that when Scott came down, washed and dressed, The Sanctuary was a hive of activity.

174

Later that morning, their new patient arrived, a fox cub, delivered by a local vet who was only too happy to break up her busy day with a cup of coffee which Scott brewed for all of them, with a cup of hot milk for Lauren.

'What's wrong with her?' asked Kimberley. She had looked up all the references to foxes the night before and felt reasonably up to speed with them. But when she saw this one, limp and lifeless and able to move her back legs but not her front ones, she was at a loss to know what was wrong.

'At first I thought she'd had an accident, so many of them come to grief on the roads,' the vet said, 'but I felt all down her spine and there didn't seem to be any damage, although she is very thin.'

'Who brought her in?' asked Scott.

'Some people up the road. They thought maybe she'd lost her parents and was too young to look after herself, but when they approached her and she didn't run away, they knew there was something more serious happening. I gave her some anaesthetic and a drip to get her fluid levels up. It was then I got my first good clue as to what was really wrong.'

'And what was that?'

'She has an infection in her ear. Ear infections can be very serious for a small animal like this. It often causes them to go around in circles as they lose their balance. But now I've administered an anti-inflammatory, she's well on the way to recovery. All she needs is several days' peace and quiet and regular feeding and she'll be as right as rain. Give me a ring if anything crops up and I'll come straight down, but for now, I'll leave her in your hands.'

'Of course. We're happy to have her, aren't we, Lauren?'

Kimberley turned around, but Lauren was already out in the intensive care area at the back of the house, checking that the fox cub was settled.

A Spoiled Sunday

'I have to admit, I had my doubts about that girl when I first saw her. She seemed a bit sullen and unfriendly', Scott said. He had his arm around Kimberley and they were strolling along the cliffs, with the moonlight shining on a coal black sea.

'I have a feeling she's had some sort of tragedy,' Kimberley told him. 'Her father completely clammed up when I started to ask about why she didn't speak — all he would say was it was a long story. I think it's done her the power of good just to be brought out of herself and given some responsibility. And I do think this place, The Sanctuary, is a very healing environment for everybody. I know I always feel different as soon as we get on the ferry. I can feel myself relaxing, and the tension seems to get blown away in the sea breezes.'

Scott stopped and turned Kimberley to him. As he looked down at her, his handsome face was bathed in moonlight and it was at times like this that Kimberley felt a warm glow, knowing he was her husband. He stroked her hair. 'It is quite a magical place. Do you remember when we were at uni together, we talked about the future and what we'd do with it?'

'Yes,' Kimberley said, wondering where this conversation was going.

'And do you remember that we talked about being successful and that if we really hit the heights in our careers we would retire early?'

'I do.'

'Well, that's what I'm working towards, Kimberley. If the Tavistock deal goes as well for me as it seems to be, our dream could become a reality.'

'Maybe it could, Scott.'

'You don't sound very sure.'

'It's just that, well, I can't help thinking that if you keep going the way you are, you'll simply not be able to enjoy an early retirement. I've never seen you sleep so much, Scott, it's like you're absolutely worn out. And I know you're not eating properly.'

'Nonsense. I'm as strong as an ox. Honestly, I'm fine, Kimberley, don't worry about me.'

★ ★ ★

On the way back to The Sanctuary, they discussed exploring the island the following day. There was a yachting marina where they could go for lunch and there was a film on at the local cinema they had missed when they were in London. That night, as she lay between newly-laundered sheets and smelt the freshness of newly-washed curtains at the window, Kimberley realised she really was happiest of all when she was down here. She had constantly wondered why Cousin Grace should have chosen her for her kind bequest, and perhaps she would never know the reason. But one thing was for sure, Cousin Grace and she had very much the same idea of Paradise, although Kimberley had a husband to share it all with, unlike poor Cousin Grace.

* * *

The next morning, they were woken up by Scott's mobile.

'Who on earth would ring at this time on a Sunday morning?' Kimberley said.

Scott's voice was muggy with sleep. 'Joe, hi mate, what's up?'

Kimberley felt herself bristle at the mention of Scott's work colleague. Why on earth couldn't he let Scott enjoy at least one day away from work?

'Can't it wait?' Scott was saying. 'Oh, okay, I see, no, not at all, it's not a problem, I quite understand.'

Kimberley leaned over and put a questioning hand on Scott's shoulder, but he shrugged her off. 'No, it won't take me long, I'll be at yours by lunchtime. Yup. See you soon,' and with that he flipped down the cover of his mobile.

'What was all that about?' Kimberley wanted to know.

'I'm really sorry, darling but I've got to go back to London straight away.'

'But we'd got the whole day planned, we were going to have lunch and everything.'

'I know, but we can do that another time, can't we?'

'I suppose so.'

'I'll make it up to you, I promise.'

'What's so important it can't wait?'

'Our American counterparts have decided to come over unexpectedly. They're due to arrive tomorrow and all the contracts have to be ready so we can negotiate terms over the next few days. There are a bunch of things they've raised queries about.'

'Scott,' Kimberley's deep brown eyes were full of concern, 'you need some rest.'

'There'll be plenty of time for rest when this deal's done and dusted.'

'But there won't, Scott. There'll be another deal after this, and another. They pay you a fortune but you never have time to spend it, so what's the point?'

'Us is the point, Kimberley, I'm doing this for us.'

It was only once he had gone that Kimberley realised he had taken the car, without any thought of how she was going to get back to London tonight.

* ★ ★

Kimberley walked over the cliffs with Ben, to the town which nestled in the next bay. She picked up a few groceries, but her heart wasn't in it, particularly as she was conscious of all the couples arm in arm, enjoying a peaceful Sunday together, and she made her way back as soon as she could.

'At least you haven't deserted me,

Ben,' she said, as she unlocked the front door. She checked her mobile, which she had forgotten to take with her, and found an anguished voicemail message from Scott. 'Darling, I'm so sorry, I was in such a hurry this morning, I never thought about how you would get back without the car. Please take a taxi to the ferry and then a train and you must take a taxi from Waterloo back to the flat. Love you lots, darling. See you later.'

She tossed the phone down on the settee.

* * *

Kimberley saw to the animals and decided the fox cub was looking much brighter, and was standing for small amounts of time. He was also eating well.

The animals took up so much of her attention that, thankfully, she didn't have time to think about Scott. By three o'clock, she realised she hadn't even thought about lunch. She resolved to do one more thing before she sat down, which was to write up the weekend's events in Cousin Grace's journal. She had carried on with all the notes on the animals' progress, exactly where Cousin Grace had left off, and Kimberley hoped that the old lady, who she felt was a constant presence, helping her with her work, would have been pleased.

Just as Kimberley was about to go into the lounge, though, the phone rang.

It was Zach Coen's unmistakably gravely tones. 'Hi, how are you?'

'Hi, Zach. I'm fine, thanks.' There was a moment's silence. Kimberley wondered if there was something wrong with Lauren.

'Umm,' Zach said, 'I was just wanting to ask you . . . you and your husband, if you'd like to come round for something to eat later on. I've been wracking my brain trying to think of some way to say thank you for spending time with

Lauren yesterday.'

'She had a wonderful day and spent the whole evening drawing pictures of animals. It was just like it used to be before . . . well . . . before our problems.'

'Oh, that would have been nice, but Scott's been called back to London unexpectedly,' Kimberley said.

'So what are you doing for dinner?'

'Nothing, actually.'

'Well, the invitation's still open. Lauren suggested it. It was either that or buy you a present but we honestly didn't know what to get you, so dinner seemed a much better idea. I'm a chef, you see, so I can rustle up a pretty good meal.'

Kimberley looked at the bag of meagre provisions she had picked up earlier for dinner on her own, and said, 'That would be lovely. What time?'

'We tend to eat early because of Lauren. How does five o'clock sound?'

'Great. I'll see you then.'

When she put the phone down, she

felt suddenly lighter in spirits. Dinner with Lauren and Zach would be so much nicer than rattling around here on her own and it was really sweet of them. Kimberley decided just to have a coffee and a biscuit to keep her going and went with much more of a spring in her step into the lounge to write up her journal.

★ ★ ★

In the bookcase there was a stack of journals bound in red leather. She took down the newest one and detailed the progress Ben was making, his new increased girth measurement and the rapid gain in weight she had found when she put him on the scales this morning. Then she charted the fox cub's treatment and was quite pleased with herself at sketching in a little picture of the cub which made her chuckle, as she was no artist. Cousin Grace, on the other hand, thought Kimberley, as she looked back through the old journals, was a considerable artist. She had decorated her journals with extremely appealing line drawings, sketches which really brought the animals to life. This was obviously one of the ways Cousin Grace filled up her many hours alone, and Kimberley was touched by the immediacy and honesty of the simple drawings showing the animals wrapped in blankets with soulful eyes one minute and, a few pages later, looking, in some cases literally, bright-eyed and bushy tailed.

As she examined the journals, she discovered that, hidden behind the red leather journals were some bound in green. Kimberley took a couple of the green journals out, opened one, and was surprised to see that it had no pictures of animals but instead was dotted with line drawings of a wonderful looking young man with laughing eyes and a generous smile. His suit was slightly old fashioned and his tie too wide and as Kimberley started to read the text, she realised that this must be

Cousin Grace's personal diary and the drawings must be of Tomasso who, Kimberley remembered, had been Cousin Grace's fiancé.

Kimberley took out all the red bound journals and found twelve of the green ones behind them, carefully dated on the spines. If Kimberley's supposition was right, she had found Cousin Grace's own personal history. Time was getting on, and Kimberley was conscious of the fact that she should shortly be at Zach and Lauren's and that she must at least change and run a brush through her hair. But she couldn't bear to put the diaries down just yet, so she flicked quickly through them to get an idea of what was in them.

The first few were written in a breathless style by a very young woman, then they matured as the years went on and the pictures of Tomasso became less and less. Kimberley followed the dates as they progressed through the years. She looked at her watch and realised she really must start getting ready. She piled the diaries on the desk in the corner, in date order, and resolved to read them when she got back.

Her heart beat suddenly faster, as she realised that here, in these hidden diaries, might lie the secret of Cousin Grace's bequest to her.

Dinner With Zach And Lauren

Kimberley turned up on Zachary Coen's doorstep clutching a bottle of wine. She had decided that with all that was going on, she couldn't possibly travel back to London tonight. Besides, what would be there for her? Scott would be at the office or, if he was back home, he would be exhausted and fast asleep. So, she would set off tomorrow morning and still be able to be back for lunchtime to see to her calls and e-mail.

'Come in!' Zach welcomed Kimberley and examined the label on the wine. 'A white Zinfandel, brilliant. That will go perfectly with the lobster salad.'

'Lobster? Goodness, you shouldn't have gone to such trouble.'

'Down here,' said Zach, showing Kimberley through to the front room, 'lobster comes a lot cheaper than it does in London. That is, if you know the right people. And as I know the guy who owns the lobster pots, I know just the right person.'

Lauren gave Kimberley a huge hug, while she threw her father a mock frown. 'Yes, I know Lauren, you don't eat lobster because you're a vegetarian, so I've done you a nice salad with chickpeas and bread.'

'I don't know quite how to put this,' Kimberley began, 'but I didn't just bring wine, I brought something, or rather someone else, with me. But as I was rushing down the path, I wasn't sure whether I should have done. It was a bit presumptuous of me.'

Zach looked at her enquiringly. 'Who else did you bring with you?'

'He's outside.' Kimberley led them out and there, sitting patiently where she'd tethered him to a fence post, sat Ben, with a red bow tied to his collar as 'evening dress' and slapping his tail expectantly on the ground. Lauren immediately went to undo his lead and took him into the house.

'Well,' Zach grinned, 'I think that settles the question as to whether he was welcome or not.'

* * *

For starters, Zach had prepared a wonderful dish of spinach and ricotta ravioli in a cream sauce. The lobster salad to follow was perfect, fresh and light after a rich starter. Finally, for dessert, they had tall glasses filled with a delicious crumble base layered with mango coulis and mascarpone, topped off with a lace fan of chocolate.

'Wow,' declared Kimberley, leaning back in her chair, 'that is by far the best meal I've had in ages. You must have been some chef, Zach.'

'I've worked in Paris, Rome, Madrid, most of the European capitals, including London. Although it's hard work, the pay is good, and I'd saved up enough to come here when we needed to . . . well . . . to rest a while.'

Throughout the meal he'd chatted

about the house they had in London and had rented out, and the inhabitants of the cove, and the tutor who came every day to teach Lauren, but this was the first time he had alluded to the problems that had brought them to Highview Cove.

Throughout the meal, Lauren had listened attentively and laughed when her father had made jokes. Now, though, she was looking restless, and so was Ben, who had stayed as good as gold, slumbering in front of the fire. 'He's ready for his evening walk,' said Kimberley. At which, Lauren leapt up and grabbed Ben's lead with an expression that said she was only too eager to take him.

'Okay then,' said Zach, 'as long as it's all right with Kimberley, it's all right with me. Kimberley and I can have coffee and watch you from the patio doors.'

'Of course,' said Kimberley. 'I think I'm too stuffed to move anyway, and Ben does so love his walk on the beach.'

Lauren ran off to put on a warm coat and scarf, kissed her father, hugged Kimberley and shot out with Ben bounding at her heels.

'She's a good girl,' said Kimberley, nursing her coffee and sitting on the comfy sofa overlooking the failing light settling on the sea and sand.

'She is indeed,' Zach said. 'But you must be wondering what's up with us two. Why we're living here in this out-of-the-way place and why Lauren has shut up like a clam.'

Kimberley fixed him with an enquiring gaze, 'Well, I can't deny it, Lauren intrigues me. She should be like other teenagers, knocking around, chatting about the latest clips on You Tube and discussing which tunes to load on to her i-pod. But obviously, something, somewhere's, gone wrong.'

Zach was silent for a moment and looked to Kimberley as though a wave of sad memories had suddenly washed over him. Then, decisively, he got up and lifted a photograph out of a drawer.

It was of a very beautiful young woman with an engaging smile. Long blonde wavy hair just like Lauren's flowed over her bronzed shoulders like a waterfall and she looked confidently into the camera. Sitting beside her was Lauren, with her head resting on the woman's shoulder. On her other side sat Zach, looking a little younger but only because his face in the photo betrayed none of the lines of worry which played around his eyes today. 'My wife, Serena, Lauren's mother.'

Kimberley took the photograph. 'She's very beautiful.'

'She was a model, but when she married me, she'd taken to dress designing and had her own company. She was doing really well, there was interest in the fashion houses of Paris and London. She had real flair.'

'But she's not around any more?'

Zach was pacing up and down the room, his coffee left to get cold. 'We had problems, she and I. Not at first, at first it was bliss, sheer Heaven. We were both struggling to make a living and were as poor as church mice but so, so happy. I'd get the odd engagements in hotels and restaurants to supplement my income when I was at catering college. She'd get a few modelling assignments, nothing big — a catalogue here, a magazine shoot there. Then Lauren came along and our world seemed totally complete.'

'So what happened?'

'In a nutshell, success. Isn't that weird?' Zach pushed his fingers through his unruly curls. 'You strive and push to get to a certain place in your life but as soon as you get there, the goalposts change. Serena was as beautiful as ever after Lauren came along, more so in fact. Having a baby seemed to turn her into something more vital, she seemed to ripen like a peach warming in the sun. She was spotted by an agency and they started giving her photoshoots abroad in wonderful places — the Maldives, the Seychelles. Meanwhile, I'd finished college, and from scraping around doing second rate jobs, I landed on my feet in a new restaurant which became the Place to Be of the fashionable set. I was in demand, I was headhunted, it was all I'd ever wanted. We managed to look after Lauren between us, with a nanny, but little by little we found that weeks had passed by and we hadn't seen each other. Serena was often abroad and I was working the most ridiculous hours, not finishing at the restaurant until two in the morning, and having to catch up on my sleep during the day.'

Kimberley felt uncomfortable listening to Zach as she looked out to the beach where Lauren was throwing sticks for Ben. Listening to him was like holding a mirror up to her and Scott's marriage.

Zach's voice came back to her. 'It must be difficult for you to understand what it's like to start drifting apart. I've seen you and Scott walking arm in arm in the evenings. You seem so close.'

'Actually,' said Kimberley, 'I think I

know exactly what you were going through.'

'That's because you're very under-standing and sympathetic and you have the ability to think yourself into someone else's shoes. I've seen those qualities in you when you interact with Lauren. But I don't think anyone can quite understand how easy it can become to concentrate on work and let a relationship slide, like Serena and I did. The only good thing was that we managed to hide the worst of it from Lauren. Maybe we shouldn't have, maybe we should have allowed her to see some of the rifts develop, so that when the crisis came it wouldn't have been such a shock to her. But it has been a terrible shock, a devastation, which, when it happened, knocked her so hard that from that instant, she hasn't said a word.'

'Have you tried to get some treatment for Lauren?'

Zach turned troubled eyes on her. 'I've tried everything. Lauren has been to the finest doctors in London, she's had endless counselling and therapies until I think she got sick of cold, clinical professionals trying to tease some sort of reaction out of her. The one thing I think she needs to do in relation to her mother is to talk about what happened, but that's the one thing she can't seem to do. Something that seems to have resulted in some sort of spark of life in her is coming here and, most of all, being with your animals. Look at her now with Ben. Seeing that gives me some hope we can move towards her recovery.'

At this point, Kimberley asked Zach a direct question. 'What did happen to Lauren's mother, Zach?' Silence hung in the air, and then Zach whispered, 'She died, in a car crash. You see,' he flopped down in the sofa, as if exhausted, 'we'd had a terrible day, one of the worst. But I guess I need to start at the beginning . . . '

★ ★ ★

While Zach spoke, and spilled out the tragic story of how he had lost his beautiful, talented wife and how Lauren had lost her mother, Kimberly sat in silence.

Every now and then her eyes strayed to Lauren, playing with Ben in the half light of the evening, and her heart went out to the girl. From everything Zach had said, Serena had loved Lauren so much and Lauren had returned that love. But, as Zach explained the circumstances leading up to Serena's accident, Kimberley could see that her head had been turned by people who didn't have her best interests at heart. The path Serena had chosen to go down had led directly to her death.

Zach had just finished telling Kimberley the details of the accident when they heard Lauren at the door with Ben. Putting on a great act of being light-hearted after all the pain he had gone through in recalling the terrible tragedy of his wife's death, Zach greeted Lauren as if he and Kimberley had been talking about nothing more pressing than the weather. Kimberley struggled not to let her feelings show about Zach's tragic story. She looked at her watch. 'I think I'd better go now, it's getting late. Can I help with the washing-up?'

'No thanks,' Zach said, 'we'll pile it all in the dishwasher and then Lauren will empty it for me. That's how she earns her pocket money and she might even get a bonus this week as we're probably going to run to three loads after tonight's dinner!'

'It's been wonderful.' Kimberley shook Zach's hand warmly and, turning to Lauren, was rewarded with the girl hugging her and kissing her cheek. Lauren had looked happy all evening and the only moment of sadness was when she had to wave goodbye to Ben.

As Kimberley made her way carefully down the darkened seaside path, an idea suddenly struck her which might be the first step on the way to recovery for Lauren. But Kimberley needed to talk it through with someone, and the best person for that would be Florence Wise.

'Come on, Ben, let's go and see Florrie.' Kimberley set off for Florence's house where, she was delighted to see, the lights were still on.

Kimberley Is Annoyed With Scott

The next morning Kimberley woke early, her mind buzzing, eager to put her plan into action. She had read about a new scheme which had originated in New York and had spread all over the world. Battersea Dogs' Home was doing it in London. It was a new idea of fostering out dogs and cats who needed homes. The person with the main care of the dog or cat would still be their owner, and still take the main responsibility and pay for their food and keep, but the foster carer would be able to look after the animal, take it for walks, give it cuddles and a temporary home until it was either ready to go on elsewhere or until the foster carer decided that they might keep the animal permanently. Kimberley phoned Zach and talked her idea through with him.

His only worry in taking on a pet was

how long he and Lauren were going to stay in the area. He had only ever looked on their stay at Highview Cove as a temporary measure to help Lauren recuperate and hopefully bring back her powers of speech. They still had their home in London and he needed at some point to get back to work. Throwing a pet into all that would, he had felt, only complicate things. But, when Kimberley suggested the possibility of fostering Ben out, he liked the idea immediately.

'So, if things change and Lauren starts to get better and we have to leave, you would take Ben back, or maybe we might decide to keep him, but we get the option to do either, right?'

'Yes, of course, whatever you want, you get to decide. Lauren's so good with Ben that I know he'll get all the love and attention he needs. I spoke to Florence about it and she thinks it's a great idea. If it gets off the ground, we might use it as a long term strategy to help us take more animals under the wing of The Sanctuary. Provided I visit prospective foster homes and check the possible foster parents out, I think it's much better for the animals to be in a proper home than cooped up in pens.'

'Okay, then, I'm happy to be your first pet fosterer. Do you want to bring Ben over today?'

'Yes. I'd planned to go back to London later this morning, but I'm not sure I'll make it now. There's so much to do here, I might stay another day. I'll bring Ben's bedding and food and stuff around later, if that's okay.'

'Brilliant, and in the meantime, I'll give Lauren the happy news.'

* * *

After Kimberley had put the phone down, it rang again. On the other end was a very impatient-sounding Scott. 'Who on earth have you been talking to, and where have you been, Kimberley? I got your text saying you were staying another night, but then I tried to get hold of you on the phone all yesterday evening and you weren't there, and this morning you've been engaged every time I phoned.'

'I'm sorry, Scott, I was out last night and I forgot to take my mobile with me.'

'Out where? With who?'

'Zach invited me over to dinner at his cottage.'

'Zach? You mean that overgrown hippy down the road?'

'He's not a hippy Scott, actually he's really nice and it gave me a chance to think of an idea to help Lauren.'

'What's he after, Kimberley?'

'What do you mean, what's he after?'

'He's single and available and you're a gorgeous looking woman. I'd just like to know what he thinks he's playing at.'

'Don't be absurd, Scott,' Kimberley said.

'When I see that Zach character again, I'm going to have a little word with him and tell him to keep away from my wife.'

'Scott, don't be ridiculous. I've got no interest in Zach at all, apart from the fact that he cooks a terrific meal and I was hungry. Now calm down, and let me tell you about this plan I've hatched for Lauren and Ben.'

Gradually, Scott calmed down. Kimberley couldn't believe he thought there might be something going on between her and Zach. What had their relationship come to that he could start accusing her of something she would never do? She told him tersely that she had decided she would stay another day at The Sanctuary. She had discovered there was an internet café in Rantnor where she could go later on and reply to all her e-mails.

* * *

One of the things Kimberley had been desperate to tackle at The Sanctuary were the rugs, which needed to be taken outside and heartily bashed to get rid of all the years of sand and grime.

She had hired a wet/dry vacuum cleaner for the week and although she had planned to tackle the rugs next weekend, she felt so worked up by Scott's ridiculous accusations, she immediately started rolling them up and took them outside.

There was a short, sturdy washing line at the side of The Sanctuary and she tossed the first rug over it. Taking a broom, she whacked it with all her might. The day was turning out to be blustery, and a gale was whipping up, just right for getting rid of all the dust and sand and annoyance she felt at Scott. As she beat at the rug, clouds of dust rose up and were whipped away in the wind. She clouted the rug again and again, the thwack of the broom giving her some relief from the indignation she felt at Scott's remarks.

Kimberley was in such a lather, and the wind was roaring so loudly in her ears, she hadn't heard Sigmund braying, or noticed Lauren coming up the path. The five rugs that Kimberley had already pounded lay in a pile on the path and another ten which needed doing were bundled up ready to go over the line. As Kimberley threw the next one on, she turned to see Lauren standing smiling, with a note in her hand which she held out towards Kimberley.

Kimberley suddenly realised she must look a bit like a mad woman in her old jeans, over-sized shirt and with her hair whipping around her face. She stopped, took the note and saw that it was a letter from Lauren saying her father had told her about Ben and how grateful she was to Kimberley for letting her look after him. At the end, the note said, 'and I want to do something to help you, please. I'll do anything to say thank you for letting me foster Ben.'

'Well then, Lauren,' Kimberley smiled, 'no time like the present. You can help me beat the rest of these rugs. Here, let me get you a broom and we'll do two at a time.'

Going indoors and getting a second broom, Kimberley encountered Ben, who had now finished his breakfast. As soon as he saw Lauren, he bounced over to her almost as if he knew she was to be his new mistress. After making a fuss of him, Lauren happily picked up the broom and copied Kimberley's lead, bashing away and giggling as Ben started jumping up and down, barking with excitement.

'Do you know, Lauren?' Kimberley said, whacking another rug, 'Scott had the cheek to tell me off for going out last night,' whack! 'When he was the one who rushed off to work when he had said he would spend the whole weekend here with me.' Whack! 'Men!' Whack! 'When you're older, you'll understand. Half the time they don't listen to you and the other half, they're not there.' Whack! 'Scott's been spending every waking moment on his job, as if that's the only important thing there is. He keeps on saying it's for us, that he's working for our future, but he isn't here looking after our present. We were meant to go out for lunch yesterday, we had a wonderful day planned for just the two of us and then he went off. Then, when he does condescend to phone me, all he can do is accuse me . . . '

Kimberley realised that Lauren had stopped beating her rug and was standing looking upset and Ben, who was in tune with her every mood, was standing looking up at the teenager and whimpering. Kimberley threw down her broom and came over to Lauren, whose dark eyes were misting and threatening to brim over with unshed tears. 'What is it? What have I said?'

The wind was tossing Lauren's blonde curls, hiding her face, so Kimberley gently stroked the hair off the girl's forehead and saw a tear spill down her cheek. Lauren opened her mouth and for a minute, Kimberley thought she might speak, she seemed so desperate to get her unsaid words out. But there was nothing. 'Come indoors,' said Kimberley and they walked in together with Ben sticking close to them.

Kimberley sat Lauren down at the table, and, taking the chair next to her, said softly, 'I wish you could talk to me, tell me what's wrong.'

Lauren, sniffing, nodded her head as if she too had that wish. She pulled a pencil and notebook out of her pocket and hastily scribbled on it. She pushed it over to Kimberley. 'You're not splitting up, are you?' was scrawled across the paper.

'Oh, Lauren.' Kimberley took the girl in her arms and hugged her, listening to the sobs which had finally come out. She remembered what Zach had told her yesterday, of how his and Serena's relationship had come steadily undone, like knitting unravelling. Although they had tried to keep the worst from Lauren, she had obviously been aware of it and the problems that had led to Serena rushing out of the house in a temper and driving away in anger, resulting in the crash that had killed her.

'I'm sorry, I'm so sorry.' Kimberley was beside herself with guilt. How could she not have realised that her going on about her troubles with Scott might bring back painful memories for Lauren? 'I shouldn't have gone on like that. I was stupid and insensitive.'

At that, Lauren shook her head vehemently. Clutching her notepad and wiping away her tears with the back of her hand, she scribbled,

No, you weren't. You were just being honest telling it like it was. I need people to tell me what's going on for once. I'm not a child any more. Crying's not so bad. I need to cry.

'I suppose you do,' said Kimberley, when she read the note. 'We all need to have a good cry sometimes. Do you feel better for it?'

Lauren smiled and nodded. Her eyes were dry now and Kimberley patted her hand. 'I'm so sorry about your parents. You say you want people to be honest and to tell you the truth, but your mum and dad kept their troubles from you because they wanted to protect you. All parents want to protect their children and keep them from pain, either emotional or physical.' Lauren's eyes were open wide as she listened intently to Kimberley. 'Scott and I are having our problems, it's true. He's obsessed with his work and with making lots of money, it's just how things are in London. I love this place and I find it really is a sanctuary from all that's going on up there. And I want a child, but I can't seem to have one.' Kimberley's own honesty surprised her, the words had just poured out. 'But just because we're having our problems doesn't mean anything horrid is going to happen. Marriage is like that, it's like the big Dipper, you go up, you go down, and hopefully you do it together.'

Lauren managed a smile and then Kimberley looked her straight in the eye. 'Why can't you talk, Lauren? What is it that stops you?'

Lauren sat and looked at her hands, with Kimberley's now lying protectively over them. The girl opened her mouth. Kimberley could see her trying to form the words, she could see her brow wrinkle with the effort and heard her breathe as she tried to force something out. When it didn't happen, Kimberly gently picked up the pencil and pushed the pad towards Lauren. Frustrated at her inability to talk, Lauren roughly pulled the pad towards her and started writing, 'B-e-c-a-u-s-e,' Kimberley watched her forming the letters. Somehow, even writing now seemed to be causing her a problem, 'I w-a-s t-h-e . . . '

Painfully, Lauren continued, 'O-n-e w-h-o.' But the pencil slipped from her hand. Kimberley held her gaze. 'You were the one who did what?'

Then Lauren started to shake her head, and she wouldn't stop. She started shaking it so hard, back and forth, and breathing so quickly, that Kimberley was worried she was heading for a panic attack. 'Don't worry, Lauren, it's okay, you don't have to say any more.' Lauren stopped shaking her head and picked up the pencil and crossed through the words. The lines were black and dark and nearly tore through the paper.

Kimberley decided the girl had had enough. 'It's all right, Lauren, I don't need to know. If you don't want to tell me, that's fine. Here, let's throw the paper away and forget about it.' Kimberley screwed up the note and tossed it into the bin.

Decisively, Lauren put away the pad and the pencil as if to signify that she didn't want to reveal anything else. Kimberley got up and said, 'Come on, the animals need feeding, there are a ton of rugs to beat and you can help me shampoo them, too, if you want.'

Lauren nodded and smiled.

★ ★ ★

Together, they fed the animals out in the pens at the back of the house. Then the two of them Hoovered and shampooed the rugs, delighting in seeing the colours come out as vibrant as new as the powerful steam cleaner did its work.

Lauren helped Kimberley lay the rugs out on the lawn to dry, and she helped to bring them in after lunch and lay them down in the house.

'Thank you so much, Lauren, the whole place looks so much better now. I could never have done it without your help.'

Lauren seemed to glow at the compliment and the sad, upset child of this morning had all but disappeared.

'Now, shall I get Ben's lead and you can take him home?'

Lauren nodded eagerly.

'He's looking so much better now, don't you think? His coat's coming back and it's got a really glossy sheen to it.'

As Kimberley loaded up a bag with tins of dog food and Ben's favourite blanket, Lauren brushed his coat lovingly with the brush Kimberley used just for him. She waved them goodbye and watched them trot off together down the path.

Just as she was about to go through the gate, Lauren waved, blew a kiss and mouthed, 'Thank you.'

★ ★ ★

As soon as Lauren had gone, Kimberley changed into a simple black skirt, leather boots and white polo neck jumper. Grabbing her bag, keys and a warm coat, she set off to walk over the cliffs to Rantnor. It was a scary walk, with the wind blowing hard, but it was refreshing. When she got to Rantnor, Kimberley went straight to the internet café and settled down with a cup of coffee to deal with her e-mails. Thankfully there weren't too many, and in a couple of hours she had answered every one and ordered a taxi to take her back, as she didn't fancy another walk across the cliffs in this weather.

The house seemed quiet after all the activity of the morning. Kimberley let herself in and hung up her coat. She walked into the lounge and over to the French doors to look at the waves crashing up to the shore and noticed a storm had developed out at sea. It would come over the land later on, she was sure of it. The sky was as black as pitch with threatening clouds rolling in. In The Sanctuary though, all was warm and dry, if a little chilly. Scott had made up all the fires in the fireplaces the other day, saying he couldn't bear to think of her being cold and, as she lit the kindling with a match and listened to the logs crackle into life, Kimberley felt a well of sadness gather within her.

Scott was the most caring of husbands. He had always looked after the practical things and, despite being a high-earning lawyer, he had always done his share of things around the house and in fact, seemed to find the chores relaxing.

* * *

As the fire leapt into life, Kimberley remembered Cousin Grace's personal journals which she had stacked up ready to read. The day had been so busy she had all but forgotten them. Working her way through them now, though, would be the perfect activity for a wet and stormy afternoon. Before she began she would just go upstairs, take off her boots and put on a warm cardigan against the draughts which were squeezing their way in through the windows.

As she got to the bedroom, it struck Kimberley how drab and dull the rugs looked in here. She had dealt with the downstairs rugs and her task for the next weekend would be the ones up here, she thought, kneeling down and running her hand across one of them. As she did, she spotted a magazine under the bed, tucked away on Scott's side. When she examined it, she saw it was a car magazine which featured very expensive, shiny new cars. It was open at a page where Scott had ringed the qualities of a very expensive Porsche, which the article was extolling. A Porsche! Surely Scott couldn't seriously be thinking of getting such a ridiculously expensive car! Stuck on the front cover was a postal label bearing the name, 'Joe Hatcher' and an address in Mayfair. So it was Joe who had lent Scott the magazine. And it didn't surprise Kimberley that Joe had one of the best addresses in London.

Still, it concerned Kimberley that Scott was even interested in such a ridiculously expensive status symbol as an expensive car. He certainly wouldn't be the man she'd married if he thought he needed a flashy sports car to advertise his success to the world.

Grace's Secret Is Revealed

Sipping a cup of coffee, Kimberley flipped over the first pages of Cousin Grace's personal journal and settled down to read. She felt the diaries talked to her almost as if Cousin Grace was sitting at her shoulder, smiling and remembering. The sky got darker and rain began to beat against the windows, but, warm and cosy in front of the leaping flames of the fire, Kimberley was captivated by her relative's account of her life and was finding it hard to hold back the tears:

Mummy and Pops don't care for me nearly as much as they care for Simone, and who can blame them? She is the beautiful one with the sweet nature. I am the serious one who spends too long peering short-sightedly over my books and is clumsy and stupid when they ask me to do things. If only I could be more like my sister, they would love me more. But it's too late now. They've travelled the world with Simone at their side and been happy to leave me at home. I remember overhearing Pops say that I was 'Grace by name but not by nature'. I must be grateful to Aunty Celia and Uncle Anton for taking me in, although I know that Uncle Anton thinks I am too plain ever to marry and he pushes me remorselessly to concentrate on my studies.

Reading this, Kimberley shuddered, knowing exactly how Cousin Grace must have felt. Her father had been as strict with her as he had been with Kimberley, regarding her as a disappointing daughter, when what he had really wanted was a son. Kimberley wished she had known Cousin Grace, she wished they had been closer in age. She read on, and her eyes filled with tears as she read of the day Cousin Grace met her beloved Tomasso, when she had gone to hear the talented young pianist play at the Wigmore Hall in London:

It seems strange to say any man is beautiful, but as I listened to that wonderful music pour out of his fingers, I was so enthralled I forgot to blink. Then he looked at me and smiled. People talk about love at first sight and they cheapen the phrase, but for me it was real. Sitting amongst a packed audience, I felt as if Tomasso and I were the only two people there. His eyes settled on me as he played his music. Me, the Ugly Duckling, seemed to be giving him inspiration.

After his performance, everyone got up, but I couldn't move. I sat there in my seat in the empty auditorium trying to pluck up the courage to go round to the stage door and ask for his autograph. What would I say to him? How could I approach a man like him? He wouldn't want to know me. But as I got up and turned round, there he was at the back of the auditorium. He had been waiting for me. For me! He told me later that he just had to get into the hall as soon as the performance ended and find me. Thank Heavens he did, because I would never have plucked up the courage to speak to him. As it was, the moment we met, we both knew that in some way this was going to last forever.

What happened to us was as unstoppable as a hurricane tearing through a forest. When Tomasso asked me to go with him to America, I would have given everything up there and then for love of him. But Uncle Anton stepped in. He had complete power over me, acting for my parents while they were away. I was such a mouse to let myself be bullied. It was the worst decision of my life.

Cousin Grace wrote, in volume four, of her utter despair at being made to stay behind in England by Kimberley's father, her Uncle Anton, and finish her studies, while Tomasso progressed his career. She consoled herself with the thought that they had the rest of their lives before them in which to marry and have children.

The account of the day Cousin Grace heard of Tomasso's death in the plane crash as he was coming back from America to marry her, was heart-rending and Kimberley had to stop her tears dripping on to the faded pages.

If only I had not listened to Uncle Anton. If only I had followed my heart, Tomasso and I would have been married. We would have had a glorious honeymoon in Hawaii and we would have travelled back together on a different plane. If I had been stronger, Tomasso would be alive today, we would have had children and my heart, instead of being shattered like glass, would be full and happy. I never want to see Uncle Anton again. I know he was trying to do what was best for me and it cannot have been easy to be left in charge of me. Nevertheless, although I wish them well, I do not want to see them again.

Kimberley read how the only thing that kept Cousin Grace going had been taking on The Sanctuary and looking after the animals. They, and this creaky, wind-blown old place, had been her salvation.

Then, in the last volume, Kimberley came across references to herself.

Against my better judgement, I allowed Aunt Celia to mend the rift slightly between myself and Uncle Anton. Many years spent here at my darling Sanctuary have mellowed me somewhat and helped me to forgive, if not forget. I would turn into a sour woman if I could not try and understand Uncle Anton's reasons for keeping me in England and preventing me from going with Tomasso. It has taken me a long time to accept that Uncle Anton was not the cause of my darling Tomasso's death. That the plane crash was simply an act of Fate. I am learning that there is a way to heal, although it is slow. Part of that healing process has been to invite Aunt Celia and Uncle Anton to The Sanctuary. I have to confess, though, that part of my reason for this is a desire to see their little girl. I feel sorry for that little child, knowing that Uncle Anton is her father. He always wanted a boy, as he said to me so many times. I have been wondering how he would cope with a girl. They have called her Kimberley, which I looked up. It means royal. And truly, when I met her, she did look like a little princess. She is such a lovely girl, and so intelligent. But Anton is often short with her, and doesn't have much time for her.

I offered to take little Kimberley for a walk. I took her to my favourite place, the beach. The sand is soft, so on the few times she tottled over, she didn't hurt herself. And, in any case, she is a brave little girl, full of pluck and spirit. She didn't cry once or get over-tired as small children so often do. I think she loves The Sanctuary as much as I do, and one thing I noticed was very strange. Her eyes reminded me of Tomasso's. There can be no connection, of course, the resemblance is only in my mind, but in that tiny child I saw the same spark of intelligence, the same quickness of intellect, that made me admire and love Tomasso. She could have been the child I never had.

I fear that Kimberley and I will not spend too much time together, though, as Uncle Anton and I still find it almost impossible to be together, and they do live so far away. But Celia has promised to send me her yearly family newsletter, and in there, I am sure, I will often hear about dear little Kimberley and can follow her progress from afar.

In the last journal, Grace was obviously weak and unwell, but she was still strong enough to put her thoughts on paper:

I can feel that I shall not last much longer. I am tired, so tired, that I can truly say, that when the time comes, I shall be ready. I haven't had a long life but I have had a full one. One thing that has given me much concern, though, has been what to do with The Sanctuary. I have made friends but have always been so much more wrapped up in my animals. I still often think about Kimberley and what she will do with her life. Celia's last Christmas letter gave me great cause for concern. I had hoped that by now she might have had children. But there is no sign of that. And Celia had said how hard Kimberley and her husband had both been working and how they were rapidly heading to the tops of their professions. It was no surprise to me that Kimberley had become a lawyer, she was such a bright child.

I know my time will come soon and last week, I made the decision to leave The Sanctuary to Kimberley. By leaving her this wonderful place, I hope that it will encourage her to slow down, to realise that there are more important things in life than a career and maybe, if, one day, she has a family, it might become their home. The Sanctuary has always cried out for children and it was a shame I could only ever supply it with animals. I know this is a bit of whimsy on my part, but who else would I leave the old place to? Some impersonal charity to be looked after by a shifting population of different people? No, that would not be good enough. This house needs a family and I plan to leave it one.

Then, the entries stopped. Kimberley was sobbing openly now. She felt she owed her relative a debt that would only ever be paid if she could provide the old house with the child Cousin Grace so dearly wanted for it.

But that prospect seemed as far off as ever, thought Kimberley, as she tucked the journals back in their hiding place. Scott and she were as far apart as ever. Miles apart, in fact. Perhaps The Sanctuary was actually having the opposite effect on their relationship to the one Cousin Grace had planned. No, thought Kimberley, that's nonsense. It was not the material things in life, property, houses, cars, jobs, that kept people apart. It was their own foolishness which lead to rifts. She must get back to Scott, she thought. She had already spent too long away from him.

As she was pondering on this, there was a knock at the door, and when she opened it, she was amazed to see Mark Steyning standing there, his umbrella straining against the high winds and only just keeping the worst of the squall from soaking him through. 'Why Mark,' she ushered him in, 'how lovely to see you. Is everything okay?'

'Actually,' he said as he smiled at her, 'I had to get this certificate regarding the bequest to you. You'll need it when you do your tax return. I have to confess, I could have posted it, but it gave me an excuse to come over and see how things were. I was really coming to make sure everything was all right with you.'

'Come into the lounge and dry out.'

Kimberley brewed a pot of tea, put some biscuits on a plate and carried them into the lounge, where Mark was warming himself by the fire.

'Here I was worrying about you being caught without fuel or having your roof blown away, and you're warm and cosy. I needn't have worried, need I?'

'No, I'm fine, Mark. Luckily, my husband, Scott, had made up all the fires and brought in loads of coal and wood before he left.'

'But he's not here now.' Mark looked a little concerned.

'No, he's not, he was called away

urgently on business.'

'That's a pity. Are the animals all right?'

'I checked on them a while ago, but it's about time I went to see them again.'

★ ★ ★

After they had drunk their tea, Kimberley invited Mark out to the back to see how the animals were faring in the storm. They were fine; all safely tucked up cosily in their beds. The fox cub was looking much better, and she covered him with extra straw to keep him warm.

At that point, the phone rang, and Mark said, 'As you've got your hands full there, would you like me to answer that?'

'Of course,' Kimberley said, thinking it was probably Zach with some question about Ben, as she deposited the straw in the fox's cage.

'Who was it?' she asked, as Mark came back into the kitchen.

'I hope I haven't caused any problems for you, but it was your husband, and he didn't seem too pleased to hear my voice on the phone. In fact, he was very short and rang off saying that if you ever have a free moment, can you ring. He should be at home this evening, he said.'

Kimberley knew that worry was written all over her face as Mark said, 'I don't want to pry, but is everything okay?'

Kimberley immediately excused herself and went to call Scott on his mobile and at the office but couldn't get hold of him. The non-communication felt almost like a slap in the face to her, as if Scott was avoiding her. Finally, in despair, she sat down and as the storm raged outside, she found herself pouring her heart out to Mark. Her loyalty to Scott meant that she couldn't tell Mark everything, but they were about the same age and he told her that he had had similar problems with an old girlfriend who had been very ambitious.

'It's been so good to talk to you,

Mark.' Kimberly said. 'And thank you for listening. I've been bottling all this up inside for too long.'

'I'm happy to help,' Mark said.

*   *   *

Kimberley had the feeling as she got up to show him out that Mark had something he needed to say to her. As they approached the door, Mark turned to her and said, 'To be quite honest, Kimberley, I had an ulterior motive in coming here today. I've always loved The Sanctuary, and I've always taken any opportunity to come over here. But I knew I would find you at home today. I happened to speak to Florence on the phone this morning and she mentioned you were here without Scott and I . . . well, I suppose I had rather hoped there was a lot of distance between you and him. I can't deny, Kimberley, that when you came down with your mother that day, I hoped that there might no longer be a Mr Wright on the scene. I enjoyed our day together when you came to look at The Sanctuary and I came down here today to ask if you'd have dinner with me.'

'But, hearing you sitting talking about your husband, I can see that you're very much in love with him and that I've got no place here, except as an advisor and, I hope, a trusted friend?'

The last was said as a question and Kimberley, trying not to show how surprised and shocked she was at Mark's confession, shook his hand warmly. 'Of course, Mark. And I'm not prepared to give up on Scott and myself yet.'

But as she watched Mark walk away, she worried about what on earth Scott would think after learning that she had been to dinner at Zach's and then, phoning her today, finding a man answering her phone.

That decided things for her. She must get back to London straight away to explain things to Scott. Not that there was any explaining to do, really, as she was sure he would soon realise.

Scott Jumps To Conclusions

When Kimberley got back to the flat that evening, she was delighted to find Scott there. But he was less than warm towards her. In fact, the atmosphere was icy. She found that, contrary to his usual habit, of wanting to tell her about everything that was happening at work, he was quite reticent. 'Mmmm' and 'really?' were the few words she got out of him.

She tried to fill the silence by telling him what she'd been up to after he'd gone back to London. She prattled on about cleaning the rugs because she thought it would please him to hear that she was being as good as her word and getting The Sanctuary to be much more the sort of place he'd want to spend time in. Kimberley kept talking, until she felt the conversation was turning into a monologue on her part.

'Scott, I wish you'd tell me what's wrong,' she said finally.

'I'm sorry I'm not good enough company for you.'

'What do you mean? You're always wonderful company. I've never seen you so . . . distant.'

'Distant, am I?' He got up and his blue eyes were blazing. 'How can you be so foolish, Kimberley?'

'Foolish? About what?'

'About what, she asks.' His tone had an edge of sarcasm to it. 'Isn't it obvious?'

'Well, no, Scott, or I wouldn't be asking.'

'OK. Let me spell it out for you. I have to rush back home because I want to make my career work for us and get us the things we want from life. And what are you doing? You're having dinner with some complete stranger over at his house. Someone I've never met, but someone who, according to Florence Wise, is a cross between Johnny Depp and Hugh Jackman. I don't reckon it's any coincidence he asked you over when I wasn't around.'

'But . . . '

Scott held his hand up and went on, 'Then, you forget to phone me and then, when I phone you after not hearing from you, some other guy I've never met answers your phone. So do you wonder that I'm a little, what did you call it? Oh yes, distant.'

'Scott, this is ridiculous.'

'I don't think it's ridiculous. I think I'm working all hours for our future, only to find you're drifting further and further away from me.'

'I'm drifting away from you? Who was it who planned our Sunday together and then walked out on the whole thing? Work seems so much more important to you than me, Scott, and it just seems to get worse and worse. Neither Zach Coen nor Mark Steyning are any threat to you, the threat to us is your job, and Joe Hatcher. He's the one who doesn't hesitate to ring you at weekends when he knows you're trying to have some sort of private life. Just because he doesn't have anything to go home to, he assumes you haven't. And yet you do have something, Scott. You've got me. I so want us to be at home together, but it hardly ever happens. Can you blame me for finding it nicer to be at The Sanctuary? And do you know why Mark Steyning came round to see me? To deliver some boring tax form, and do you know what else he said? He said he could see that I was so in love with my husband that the words 'not available' might as well be written across my forehead.'

'I know how wrapped up you are in your work at the moment but there are so many other things in life. The Sanctuary is the most wonderful place I've ever known. Oh, it's lovely here in our flat, but it's not really a home, is it? It's a place to sleep before rushing back off to work again.'

'It's so different at The Sanctuary. I wish you could see that. So much has happened there lately, things that will explain to you exactly why I wanted to spend time at Zach's. It's not him I'm interested in, and he's definitely not interested in me. Only a few months ago he lost his wife in a terrible car crash, poor man.'

'The only person I'm interested in in that house, is Lauren. She's such a lovely girl, but so troubled, and I think I've finally found a way to get through to her and you don't care a jot!'

'Oh, Kimberley.' Scott crashed down on to the sofa next to her and swept her up in his arms. 'I'm sorry. I'm so sorry. I've been prowling around here and at work thinking the worst. I don't know what's wrong with me; I'm jittery all the time. I'm so exhausted, but last night I didn't sleep a wink. I felt so wound up.'

'Scott, being stressed out is what's making you paranoid about what I'm doing. Everything is getting way out of proportion. Can't you see that?'

'I've been selfish and stupid. It's just that I don't want to lose you.' He took her hands and said, 'So tell me all about Lauren and this plan of yours.'

Kimberley explained to him everything that Zach had told her about Lauren and about how, this morning, Lauren had nearly told her what was troubling her. 'I'm sure I could get through to her, Scott. She was so close to telling me. I think, up till now, she's probably felt like she's being analysed by all and sundry. What she really needs is a friend, but friends of her own age wouldn't understand. I suppose what she needs most of all is a mother.'

'Be careful, Kimberley. I know you want to help her and I know you want a child desperately, but you can never be a mother to Lauren.'

'I know Scott, but how can I see someone crying out for help and not try to do something if I can see a way? The animals are the key, especially Ben.'

'You're a good, kind person, Kimberley and . . . and I'm so sorry having a child hasn't happened for us.'

Kimberley placed her finger over

Scott's lips. 'Don't talk about it, Scott. Sometimes, when you have a problem, you spend so much time thinking about it you can't get on with anything else in your life. You need a break from it. I think The Sanctuary's given me that break. Ever since I inherited that funny old place, I haven't thought so much about the baby stuff and when I have, the pain hasn't been so bad. Cousin Grace could never know it, but she's helping me in so many ways.'

Kimberley went on to tell Scott about Cousin Grace's personal journals and he was pleased she had solved the mystery surrounding her unexpected inheritance.

★   ★   ★

Kimberley had hoped that evening was going to signal them drawing closer together, but the demands that work, and Joe Hatcher, made on Scott didn't get less; in fact, they increased.

The last couple of weekends, Scott

hadn't been down to The Sanctuary at all. He had been so tied up with meetings and he'd said he didn't want to let her down by having to come back early. But she had at least got him to promise to come down one weekend every month. 'You need to get away properly,' she said. 'In fact, I think what you need is a holiday. We haven't had any time off since Christmas and it'll soon be Easter.'

The idea she had planted must have grown because one day when, unusually, they were having dinner together at the flat, Scott announced, 'You know you were talking about getting away for a proper holiday? Well, I've got a surprise for you.'

'Really?'

'Yes. I've booked for us both to go to France in a month's time. We're going to drive and go through the Channel Tunnel. You've often said you'd like to do that.'

'That sounds wonderful, Scott,' Kimberley said, but then remembered something. 'What about The Sanctuary, you do know I have to go down every week?'

'I've thought of that. We're leaving on a Monday morning and coming back on a Friday evening, so you can still have your weekend down at The Sanctuary. I know how important that it is to you. Besides, a few short days off were all I could negotiate with Joe.'

'And there's one more surprise I've got up my sleeve, but you're going to have to wait until nearer the time before I let you in on that secret,' Scott grinned.

Kimberley did everything she could try to to get Scott to tell her what the surprise was, but he just smiled and told her to wait and see.

Any time over the next few weeks when she felt down about the fact that he wasn't there, or worried when she found him up in the middle of the night pacing the lounge, or sitting wide awake ploughing through mountains of documents when he should have been asleep, she hung on to the fact that they were soon to go away for a whole five days together, and she would wonder as to what the surprise would be.

Perhaps it was to be dinner at one of the most exclusive restaurants in Paris, or maybe a trip to Monet's garden at Giverny. The wisteria would be coming out when they were there, and Scott knew she loved a birthday card he had given her once, which showed the blooms over the blue, painted bridge in Monet's garden. The wisteria looked like white foam and she so loved the image she had kept the card. That must be it, Kimberley decided, feeling her heart fill with love for Scott. He was still her caring, considerate husband.

★ ★ ★

Kimberley had enjoyed her weekends at The Sanctuary recently. All the animals were doing well and she'd managed to wash all the curtains and clean all the rugs and, doing one each weekend, had repainted all the major rooms.

When you opened the front door now the house smelt fresh and clean and when the sun poured through the windows it lit up the newly painted rooms which she'd done in a selection of different pastel shades. There was peach, primrose, rose pink, apple white and bird's egg blue. The land on the hill behind the house was sprouting with bluebells and spotted with bright yellow primroses. Truly, Kimberley felt that if it hadn't been for The Sanctuary in these difficult times she was having with Scott, she didn't think she could have coped.

One day, just as she was finishing lunch, her mother phoned. 'I'm so looking forward to our holiday, Mum,' Kimberley said. 'It's going to give us a proper chance to be together without anything getting in the way. It'll give Scott and me a chance to talk.'

'That sounds a bit heavy,' Celia said. 'Is there something particularly on your mind?'

'There is, Mum. I'm so worried about Scott. When he started this extra work, he said it wouldn't be for long, they'd just have to win the contract and then it would all settle down. But it hasn't. If anything, it's got worse. He's not just working at the office late into the evenings and being called in at weekends, he's bringing more and more work home with him. I'm worried about him. He has dark shadows under his eyes and he looks so pale.'

'Is he still going to the gym?'

'Hardly ever now, and he used to love that so much.'

'Is he eating all right?'

'He seems to exist on black coffee. The other night, I woke up at three in the morning and went into the kitchen to find him with a pile of documents and a whole cafetiere of strong coffee beside him. He couldn't have had more than four hours sleep. I'm so worried about him. I'm going to ask him if he could just think about getting another job. One that isn't so pressurised. We don't need the extra money and I'm simply not convinced he can keep this up. He's dominated by this awful guy at work, Joe, who I've never even met, who seems to run his team like a band of slaves.'

'Perhaps a holiday will help him to see sense,' said Celia, sounding as worried as her daughter.

A Mystery Is Solved

It was two weeks before they were due to go away, and for the first time in a long while, Scott had come down to The Sanctuary with Kimberley. On the Saturday morning, the phone rang, and Scott rushed to answer it as if he was expecting the call.

'Okay, brilliant. Right mate, yup, bring her down here. How long do you think you'll be? Only an hour? Of course, it won't take you long. See you then.'

'Who was that?' Kimberley asked.

'Never you mind.' Scott tapped the side of his nose. 'It's a surprise, the surprise I told you about.'

'Scott,' Kimberley laughed as he whirled her around, 'you're like a kid with a new toy, what's going on?'

'You'll see,' he said, 'in about an hour.'

Kimberley had hungry animals to feed and tend and had her sleeves rolled up and her hair tied back filling up the water bowl in one of the last pens when there was a call on Scott's mobile.

He came outside, grabbed her by the hand and said, 'Come on, come and see the surprise!'

Newly showered, with his hair damp round his face, she could see a lot of the old Scott as he laughingly dragged her up the steps at the back of the house. It reminded her of how he had been at university when their results came through; how he had held her by the hand and dragged her down to their favourite coffee shop and splashed out on the biggest, most expensive cake in the place.

Afterwards, he had given her a piggy back home, galloping across the park saying he wouldn't only be her knight in shining armour but that he was happy also to be her faithful steed. Scott had been so full of fun then, and

Kimberley was so pleased to see that today, some of that old fun was back.

★ ★ ★

When they got to the car park at the top of the steps, Kimberley saw a man in a crisp suit with a large gold watch at his wrist, and a bunch of keys dangling in his fingers, leaning on a long, sleek sports car. The man smiled broadly at Scott. The car, low on the ground, with its two seats laying back, was a bright yellow and the driver's door stood open.

'She's all yours,' the man said to Scott.

'She's fantastic. I can't wait to take her to France. Isn't she gorgeous, Kimberley?'

Kimberley looked at the car, emblazoned with the name, *Porsche*, and was speechless. She said absolutely nothing, but could feel her fingernails digging into her hand as she turned her back on Scott. Feeling the breeze cool on her hot cheeks, she went back down the steps. She could hear Scott behind her talking to the man with the keys and bidding him a hasty goodbye as he shouted after her, but she didn't look back.

As she reached the bottom of the steps, Kimberley registered the slight figure of Lauren on the beach, running around with Ben.

She could hear Scott's footsteps as he rushed down after her, calling out to her. She didn't want to speak to him, she didn't want to look at him, so that when he finally caught up with her, he had to grasp her by the shoulders and swing her round to face him.

'Kimberley, what's wrong?'

'So that was the surprise, was it?'

'Yes.'

'You thought I'd be pleased that you'd gone and spent a fortune on some ridiculous, souped up, joke of a car?'

'It's for our holiday, it'll be great, it goes really fast and it looks so good, don't you think?'

Kimberley could just make out Lauren standing staring at them. She was standing at the gate, with Ben sitting beside her. Kimberley turned to Scott and shouted at him in frustration, 'How could you go and waste our money on buying something as vain and superficial as a sports car? We'll barely even get any luggage in that thing! It'll cost us a fortune in petrol and I'd be embarrassed to be seen in it. I don't even want to know how much it cost, to know how much money you've wasted on such rubbish when we've got a perfectly good car already! You know I wasn't in favour of getting a new car and certainly not something like that! Now you'll have to work even harder and longer to pay for it. Where is it all going to end, Scott?'

'Have you quite finished?' Scott said.

Lauren who, on hearing the raised voices, had come closer, stood by, looking from Scott to Kimberley, frown lines creasing her forehead.

'Yes, I have finished,' Kimberley said through gritted teeth.

'Then I'm going for a drive in my new car. If it's of any interest to you, although I don't think you're interested in listening to anyone at the moment as you haven't let me get a word in, I haven't bought the car. I've hired it for our holiday.'

'It seems to me, Kimberley, that you're so het up and emotional lately you simply can't think straight. You misjudge me at every turn, you jump to conclusions, you're irrational, you don't listen to me. I was only going to hire the car for the week, just to make the drive to France more pleasant. But now I'm having second thoughts. I might jut as well go ahead and buy it. After all, you made the decision to take on The Sanctuary without asking me! I shall come back, maybe, when you're more rational. Or maybe I shall just drive back to London and stay there!'

He stormed back up the steps, the car keys jangling in his hand, while

Kimberley watched his retreating figure. She felt ragged, drained and distraught. She heard the gate squeak open and heard Sigmund braying, but she didn't want to speak to Lauren or anyone else. She had accused Scott when she should have given him a chance to explain.

She rushed into the house and snatched up the keys to the BMW. She'd made such a mistake, getting at him like that. She must go after him, explain that it wasn't really the car, but the stress and strain of the last few months that had made her fly off the handle.

As she flew out of the house with the car keys in her hand, she saw Lauren's face panicked with worry. But she couldn't deal with the girl's problems now, she had her own to sort out. As she ran up the steps, she could hear Lauren's quick footsteps and the tapping of Ben's paws as they ran up behind her. At the car park, she saw the empty space where the Porsche had been, and the deep indents of tyres where Scott must have hared off at a ridiculous speed.

As she tried to put her keys in the BMW, her hands were shaking so much she fumbled and dropped them. She reached down and picked them up. But then she felt her arm held. Lauren was there, desperately trying to stop her, to hold her back. Poor Ben just ran around the two of them, not knowing what to do. Kimberley shook Lauren off and said, 'For goodness' sake, Lauren, let me go.'

She saw the girl's face screw up and her mouth open. Moving Lauren firmly aside, Kimberley managed to get the car door open, but Lauren stood in her way as she tried to shut it.

'Lauren, please, I must go after him.' Kimberley struggled, pulling the door against Lauren. Lauren stamped on the ground in frustration, grasped Kimberley by the shoulder and opened her mouth yet again. She contorted her face, moved her lips and suddenly emitted a loud, 'No!'.

'What do you mean no?' Kimberley started to say, then suddenly she let out a gasp and said, 'say that again.'

'No!' yelled Lauren, 'no, no, no. Please don't. It's dangerous.' Kimberley was stopped in her tracks, hearing the girl speak for the first time. And now the floodgates had been opened, the words tumbled out like a waterfall. 'Don't go, Kimberley. You'll die, just like my mum. She ran off like this and it was all my fault.'

Kimberley closed the car door. Lauren looked truly terrified. 'What do you mean it was your fault?'

'It was my fault she ran away, my fault she got in that car, my fault she drove too fast, my fault she died.'

'Look at me,' ordered Kimberley grasping Lauren's shoulders, 'and tell me what happened.'

Lauren gulped, as if she were drowning and fighting for air. 'We'd had a row that morning, Mum and me. It was over nothing. I'd bought this skirt, you see, which she hated. It was

259

too short, and it was red and my friend had one just like it, and I loved it. Mum told me to take it off so we could take it back to the shops, but I wouldn't. She told me to stay in my room and when she went off down the stairs, I slammed my door so hard it made the pictures on the wall rattle.'

Lauren ran her fingers agitatedly through her curls. 'At first I didn't hear what was going on downstairs because I plugged myself into my iPod and played the music as loud as I could. But then, when I'd calmed down a bit, I took off the rotten skirt and put on a pair of jeans. I was going to go downstairs and say sorry, because I really was sorry.'

'But then I heard Mum and Dad talking in loud voices. I knew, I just knew, they were arguing about me. Then I heard the front door bang really loudly and I saw Mum running off towards the car. Her hair was all wild and flowing behind her and her jacket was only half on, like she didn't care how she looked or anything.'

Lauren gulped for air again.

'Go slowly, Lauren, you're doing fine.' Kimberley smiled encouragingly, still holding the girl's shoulders as if Lauren might collapse if she let them go.

Lauren breathed deeply and began again. 'I went through the front door and ran after her. But I was too late. She didn't see me, she didn't look behind her when I called. She just got into the car and screeched off. I'll never forget that sound. She was going much too fast. When I came back in, Dad looked shattered. Then we just waited for her to come back, but she never did. She was cross with me, Kimberley, that's why she ran off, that's why she died.'

'Oh, Lauren, no, no. You've got it all wrong.'

A note of hardness crept into the girl's voice. 'What do you mean, I've got it wrong? You can't know, you weren't there.'

'No, but your father was, and he told

me exactly what the argument between him and your mother had been about. The other day when I came to dinner and you were playing with Ben, your father told me everything about that day. And it had absolutely nothing to do with you.'

'I don't believe you. You're just saying that.'

'I'm telling you the truth, Lauren.' Kimberley released her hold on Lauren's shoulders and took the girl's limp hand gently in her own. 'The only reason your father hasn't told you is because he thought the truth would be too painful. The fact is, your mother was thinking of going away. She had been given the chance to do a photo shoot that would have taken her around the world for many months. But she couldn't take you with her, your schooling would have suffered too much. You'd just started secondary school and were settling in and making friends. Your father knew you would miss your mother if she went away for months on end and he'd pleaded with her not to take the job, or at least to wait until you were a bit older. She simply couldn't make a decision because she was torn between her career and her family.'

'It was no-one's fault, Lauren. It was an accident, pure and simple. Your mother was in a turmoil knowing she had a difficult decision to make and in a way, I suppose, her driving off was a way of running away from that decision. She was just buying herself a bit of time. She would have come back and everything would have been OK if she hadn't been concentrating on other things instead of on the road.'

'But why didn't Dad tell me?'

'He was worried that if he told you the argument was about your mother trying to choose between going away to work or staying to be with you, that would make you feel you were some-how second best to your mother's career. How could he know you were blaming yourself for the accident?'

'I don't know what happened to me when I couldn't speak,' Lauren said. 'I wanted to speak, I knew what I wanted to say, but the words just wouldn't come out. I guess maybe I thought that, by saying nothing, I couldn't do anything else wrong. But Ben helped me through.'

'He did?' They both looked at the dog, who sat wagging his tail expectantly.

'I could talk to him. He just listens. He doesn't judge me. I told Ben everything, all the bad stuff, everything about how I was feeling. And even when I told him the worst things, how selfish I'd been over that stupid skirt, and how I upset Mum and how it was me who caused her to crash, all he did was lick my face. Ben loves me even though I'm a horrible person.'

'You are not horrible, Lauren, don't ever say that. You're someone who's had too much to deal with in her young life. You're good and kind and helpful and your father loves you so much. He's hurting too, you know. He needs help just as much as you, and you can help each other.'

'I want to go back now and see Dad.'

'Come on, then,' Kimberley said, putting her arm around Lauren and setting off down the steps towards the cove. 'He'll be so delighted to have his little girl back.'

★　★　★

To say Zach looked like a man who'd won the lottery would be an understatement. There were hugs, kisses and tears. Kimberley left them together to make up for lost time.

Zach phoned Kimberley later in the day and poured out his thanks.

'I did nothing Zach, honestly. It was just pure luck that what happened panicked Lauren into speaking. Lauren could see the same thing happening to me as happened to her mum, and she may well have been right. I wasn't safe to drive in the mood I was in.'

'Have you heard from Scott?'

'No, I haven't and I'm worried sick. It's my fault he dashed off like that. I keep phoning but his mobile is either engaged or goes to voicemail. I've phoned the flat, too, but there's no reply.'

'I've been feeling so queasy with all the tension. I tried to clean out the cages this afternoon, but every time I bent down I felt literally sick with worry. I don't want to lose him, Zach. Scott means everything to me.'

A Dream Come True

That evening, Kimberley couldn't face the thought of eating. She thought some fresh air might do her good. Dejectedly, she put on her warmest coat and scarf and set off along the cliffs to Rantnor. She didn't know what she was going to do there, it wasn't that busy at the best of times, and everything was closed except the pub. She went inside, but the musty, beery smell of it made her stomach churn and she quickly ordered a sparkling water. Once she had drunk that, feeling a little better, she made her way back along the cliffs.

It was a starry night, clear and breezeless with a full moon shining on the waves below. Feeling suddenly not just tired but exhausted, Kimberley stopped and looked out over the sea. The waves rolled in and out on the beach below and she listened to them sighing like some great sleeping sea creature breathing in and out. She pulled her coat tight around her and wondered if she would ever feel Scott's arms about her again. Would they ever find a path in life that they could walk together? It seemed impossible after what had happened today, and she had never felt so alone.

Then, in the darkness, lit by the sheen of the moon, she became aware of a figure running along the cliff from The Sanctuary. She didn't dare hope it might be . . . but then, as he came closer, she couldn't mistake that tall figure, those shoulders full of strength. Scott was running towards her.

She turned to face him as he caught up to her and wrapped her in his arms. She felt the warmth of his body, the slight roughness of his chin against her cheek.

'I'm so glad I found you, darling.' His words seemed to flow through her, warming her, melting away the sadness and hurt.

'Scott, I was so desperately worried about you. How can I tell you how sorry I am? I shouldn't have made such a fuss about the car. I don't care if you want to buy a Porsche or anything else. I just want you.'

'Kimberley, the last thing I want is a sports car, I promise you. I only thought it would be a bit of fun, and get us down to France quicker. But the fact that I even considered it and wasn't satisfied with the BMW, made me think. That, and the news I got today, not long after I left you.'

'What news?' Kimberley felt herself stiffen. Had he been promoted again? Did they perhaps want Scott to take over one of their offices abroad? What was going to disrupt them and threaten them now? A thousand possibilities deluged Kimberley like thunder clouds raining on her hopes that they could be together.

Scott stroked her hair. 'When I left you I didn't know where to go. I knew I'd overreacted and I hadn't really meant to go back to London, but I headed towards the ferry terminal anyway, just for somewhere to go. When I was there, leaning on the car, staring at all the happy people coming over for day trips, and feeling miserable, my mobile rang. It was my secretary, Delia. She was in a complete state and didn't know what to do.'

'Joe Hatcher's had a massive heart attack.'

Kimberley stared at Scott.

'The hospital phoned Delia because he had a list of phone numbers in his wallet. They were all work colleagues and ex-wives and old girlfriends and they just worked through the list. Poor Joe. The hospital had tried three of his old girlfriends but none of them would go to see him. Joe isn't that good at breaking up with people.'

'Delia asked me if I'd go and see him and I just didn't feel I could say no. I got straight on the ferry and drove up to London as fast as I could. I tried to phone you, but the battery ran down on my mobile on the ferry and the payphone in the harbour had a great long queue. I thought I would phone you from the hospital, but when I got there, the public phone wasn't working, and I had to go in to see Joe. Kimberley, it was touch and go for him.'

'Is he going to be all right?'

'The doc's told him he needs a quadruple bypass. They've also told him if he doesn't lay off the ciggies, booze and strong coffee and find himself a less stressful job, he's not likely to see another Christmas. But do you know what the saddest thing is?'

'The only people they could find who would visit him were people from work. I was there for an hour with him, before one of the other guys arrived, then I rushed back to you. We felt a bit odd being there. He should have had family around him, a wife, children, parents, something. But the guy doesn't have anyone. He lives, eats and breathes work.'

Scott took Kimberley's hand in his. 'Kimberley, I don't ever want to be like that. I don't ever want to be some mega-successful guy with fast cars and a fast lifestyle but with no-one in the world who cares about him. I've been stupid and vain. I drank up the power of success at work, and I was beginning to love the money, too. But you can lose all that in a second. When I went to see Joe, he just looked like a sad, lonely, middle-aged man with more money in the bank than he knows how to spend. What does all that mean if you don't have your health and people who love and care about you?'

'Oh, Scott, I love you just as much now as I always have. I felt I was losing you, but now you're coming back.'

Scott placed his lips tenderly on hers and kissed her in the way he had when he had proposed to her and she'd said yes. She felt as if she were floating in his arms as the ebb and flow of the waves below matched the pounding of her heart.

As they walked hand in hand back to The Sanctuary, Kimberley told Scott about Cousin Grace's diaries. 'This place has been a lifeline to me while we've been so far apart, Scott,' she said. 'Cousin Grace lost her love and I was in danger of losing mine, but I think, now, with her help, we've come together again.' Then, remembering the events of earlier in the day, she told him excitedly about Lauren. Scott was delighted for her and said that he'd like to get more involved with the people living in Highview Cove.

As they got inside The Sanctuary, and Scott went into the kitchen, he saw the straw and bedding for the animals scattered on the floor where Kimberley had left it when she'd felt ill.

Kimberley had gone into the lounge, tired after her walk, so Scott put everything to rights, putting the night-time bedding into the cages so the animals could get settled down. 'What's been going on here, you've always been so conscientious with the animals. Are you all right?' he asked, seeing Kimberley lying on the sofa, not even having taken her boots off.

'I don't know what's wrong with me. I feel so exhausted. And the smell of the animal food seems so strong I have to hold my breath when I open the tins. Maybe they've changed the recipe or something.'

'I think you need to get yourself up to bed, you've been overdoing things as much as I have. And walking across windy clifftops may have given you a chill.' He lifted her up in his arms and she linked her hands happily around the back of his neck and laid her head on his shoulder as he carried her upstairs.

The next morning, Scott insisted that Kimberley stay in bed. 'You could have a cold or have caught some tummy bug or something, so you're just going to stay there and let me look after you.'

Kimberley snuggled back down

under the covers and lay supremely contented in bed, with the morning sunshine streaming through the windows, warming her. Scott brought up a fresh pot of tea and two toasted currant buns which she tucked into. 'This is bliss, Scott. I was absolutely starving.'

'You had hardly anything to eat yesterday, so it's not surprising.'

Scott watched her, deep in thought, as she wolfed down the buns. 'D'you know what? I'm going to toast you some more.'

He brought up a further three currant buns and they all disappeared, after which Kimberley slumped back on the pillow and said she couldn't eat another thing.

'Right. You just stay here and get your strength back. I don't want you catching anything before we go off to France. I'm going to go into Rantnor to get a paper and we've run out of fresh fruit and veg for the animals. I'll pop into the chemist and see if I can get you some sort of pick-me-up, too.'

Two hours later, Scott came upstairs bringing one of his shopping bags with him. 'How are you feeling?'

'So, so. But much better for having had some sleep.'

He took a carton of orange juice out of his bag, some multivitamins and a small blue and white box. He gave her an enigmatic look as he pointed to the box. There was a strange glint in his eye as he said, 'I think you ought to do something with this.'

She picked the box up. 'A pregnancy test?'

'That's right.'

'No, Scott, I can't do it. Why on earth did you get it?'

'Don't be such a total dope, Kimberley,' he chided her gently. 'Your mind's been concentrating so much on other people lately you haven't had a chance to think about yourself. You're an intelligent lawyer, you're used to looking at the facts.'

Scott sat down at the side of the bed

and said, 'Let's tick them off one by one. You're exhausted, you've been feeling queasy and off-colour, you can't bear intense smells and you're eating twice as much as old Sigmund out there. You're either turning into a donkey with a bad tummy upset or . . . you're pregnant.'

Kimberley's eyes widened as she looked at the box. 'I'm not sure if I can do this, Scott. What if it's bad news? I can't take any more disappointment. Let's just leave well alone.'

'We have to face things, Kimberley. And I'm here with you. Whether it's good news or bad, we're in it together, I promise you that.'

★ ★ ★

Ten minutes later, Kimberley came back into the room to find Scott sitting with his head in his hands. He jumped up, trying to look calm, but she could tell he was anxious.

He dragged his fingers through his

already messed-up hair. 'Well?' he croaked.

'Well,' Kimberley said, a smile flickering at the corners of her mouth.

'Kimberley, don't do this to me, what did the test say?'

Kimberley swallowed. 'I'm — we're — going to have a baby.'

Scott's whoop as he lifted her up in the air and swung her round could have been heard on the mainland. She saw a tear appear at the corner of his striking cornflower blue eyes and when he had put her down, she wiped it away tenderly.

Scott immediately went downstairs and picked up the phone, dialling again and again, speaking to everyone in his phone book. His laughter bubbled up the stairs as Kimberley put on her dressing gown and opened the French windows of the bedroom. Standing on the balcony overlooking Highview Cove, she bathed in the glittering sun which played across the gentle waves of the sea. Sigmund was munching contentedly on the grass, his hooves nestling among yellow primroses. Out on the sand she could see Lauren playing with Ben, and as the girl looked over, Kimberley gave her a wave.

Thanks to Cousin Grace, thanks to this funny old house and this heavenly bay, she had found her heart's desire. Her hand went down and rested on her tummy. Something about being here, putting her energies into doing up this beautiful home, caring for the animals and the people who lived here, and something about getting away from the frantic madness of the city, had nourished her spirit and her body. The Sanctuary had given her and Scott the one thing they most wanted in the world. They truly had found their Paradise, here on earth.

We do hope that you have enjoyed reading this large print book.

Did you know that all of our titles are available for purchase?

We publish a wide range of high quality large print books including:
Romances, Mysteries, Classics
General Fiction
Non Fiction and Westerns

Special interest titles available in large print are:
The Little Oxford Dictionary
Music Book, Song Book
Hymn Book, Service Book

Also available from us courtesy of Oxford University Press:
Young Readers' Dictionary
(large print edition)
Young Readers' Thesaurus
(large print edition)

For further information or a free brochure, please contact us at:
Ulverscroft Large Print Books Ltd.,
The Green, Bradgate Road, Anstey,
Leicester, LE7 7FU, England.
Tel: (00 44) **0116 236 4325**
Fax: (00 44) **0116 234 0205**

THE ORANGE MISTRESS

Sara Judge ELENOR

Alice Wingard tells the story of how Nell Gwyn saves her from destitution when she is orphaned. Nell takes her to live in a bawdy house in Coal Yard Alley. The well-educated Alice finds her new surroundings shocking. Yet the girls' friendship deepens as, together, they move on from the theatre in Drury Lane, to Pall Mall and then to the court of the lascivious Charles II. Sharing happiness and sorrow, they encounter bloodshed, passion and political intrigue . . .